M000190578

OUR PLAGUE

OUR PLAGUE

A NOVEL OF ABSURD FICTION

CHERYL PERICH

Charleston, SC
www.PalmettoPublishing.com

Our Plague: A Novel of Absurd Fiction

Copyright © 2022 by Cheryl Perich

All rights reserved. No part of this publication may be reproduced, stored or transmitted in any form or by any means, electronic, mechanical, photocopying, recording, scanning, or otherwise without written permission from the publisher. It is illegal to copy this book, post it to a website, or distribute it by any other means without permission.

This novel is entirely a work of fiction. The names, characters and incidents portrayed in it are the work of the author's imagination. Any resemblance to actual persons, living or dead, events or localities is entirely coincidental.

Cheryl Perch asserts the moral right to be identified as the author of this work.

Designations used by companies to distinguish their products are often claimed as trademarks. All brand names and product names used in this book and on its cover are trade names, service marks, trademarks and registered trademarks of their respective owners. The publishers and the book are not associated with any product or vendor mentioned in this book.

None of the companies referenced within the book have endorsed the book.

First Edition

Paperback ISBN: 978-1-68515-857-6
eBook ISBN: 978-1-68515-858-3

Contents

Chapter 1

The events of that year were that of the unusual. In Denver, while faces were largely masked and hidden, the masks themselves became banners announcing the abnormalities of our plight. Before this year, the city was nothing out of the ordinary—a city big enough to get lost in, but small enough to retain a unified character. Now its character is void of convocation, replaced with pestilence.

From afar the ground violently juts into the sky providing contrast to the quadrated buildings. The buildings formed a crooked toothy smile of blues, sandy red, and silver. The city has a cool, crisp air that seems to gently pull on your skin with each breeze. It's almost a negative pressure, an absence of place. Like a single air bubble making its way upward through water. A last breath.

The air reminded me of Albuquerque, though Denver was nothing more like it. There the landscape seemed as if it was painted on a curtain at the edge of the world—edge in that the town was so isolated from the rest of the world that it broke away from the larger sphere. Like a tiny chip in a marble. There were seasons there, as there are here in Denver, but they were subdued. This made its inhabitants feel as if they lived outside of time, on the edge of nothingness, and hauntingly still. It was there I learned of the absurd.

Ignorant of the seasons, the sun in Colorado blazes. Gossamer wisps of air stand no match against it. It brings about a mutual understanding of the fragility of life. The falls, though not having the bright bursts of red, green, and orange of my midwestern childhood, were firework shows of saturated yellow Aspen leaves sparkling in the blue sky. Winters annealed the landscape with soft snow, which never tainted yellow or brown before disappearing as quickly as it came. The city slows without street sweeping, and the only venture-fixated escape it is to skirt the cliff edges. The city felt like it had earned its place next to the great peaks. Factories and warehouses maintained the industrial feel and a nod to its past, while the glass skyscrapers mirrored the pastel Colorado sunset. Hard and soft, light and dark, rough and smooth, the city gracefully balanced oppositions.

To know the people, you need to understand the land. The beauty mesmerizes those keen to avoid temperature control and barriers to the austerity beyond. The people numb themselves with the silence of the wood and the vastness of the open space. Similar, again, to other cities, where instead of the outdoors propensity, they indulge in the night and its vibrant strokes. The men here all own dogs, large and sloppy. The women are all fit and svelte from hiking and skiing, rock climbing, and mountain biking. Instead of waiting in lines at bars, those in this town waited in caravans of Subarus on I-70 W, all desperate for something to fill the vacuum. I didn't exactly fit in with such outdoorsy folk, but I could appreciate their instinct to escape.

Such being the normal life of Denverites, it would be easily understood that we had not the faintest ability to apprehend the events that took place. They were premonitory signs of what I shall describe had followed. The transition from pre to post happened to almost all of us in our own way. Left behind were the non-believers, but it was assumed they'd meet their end. What met us was a time of plague—a plague of disease, of misinformation, conspiracy, and division.

Chapter 2

Leaving my office, I slipped lightly feeling my balance shift to and from erratically. Arms thrown out, I steadied myself and paused to study the source of this dizziness. An orange mold thinly veiled the surface of the sidewalk. It was a violent orange, reserved for that of caution or the audacious 80s. It lightly dusted the sidewalk square below my feet, dissipating at the edges. Bent over gazing curiously at the aberration, I was distracted by the ping of my cellular device.

I stood up abruptly and consummated the summons by checking my phone. Social media claimed it was my college roommate's sister's birthday and suggested I wish her well. I cycled through this and other media apps absently, scanning the scandal-ridden headlines. Most headlines boasted proof of government-backed radicalized extremism or abstract leadership's dabbles into pedophilia—all quite typical of a growing mass adherence to conspiracy theory. Instead, I paused on an article regarding a respiratory illness discovered in China. Symptoms included trouble breathing, fever, shaking, and ocular discoloration. It seemed to be spreading quickly and there was much unknown about the mechanisms. Growing disinterested in details of something so far removed from my current plights, I continued towards my car. The mold took a deep breath in and out, expelling with it nodules of aspirated expiry.

Only as I marched across the parking lot did I notice Michael's presence. Michael seemed focused and hunched, as I was moments ago. As it was his job to maintain the occupational environment, the presence of this mold distraught him and struck him as odd. I mentioned to him my encounter with the very same orange dust at the landing. Michael only shook his head in disbelief as he had yet to see something similar or familiar in the growth.

"Strange color," Michael grunted softly.

"Indeed," I replied. "Do you know what it is? What it might be?"

Michael coughed lightly, then poured a bucket of water over the mass to dissipate its presence. The vibrant orange cloud swirled toward the gutter, drifting past my feet. I noticed then a few specks of orange on my shoes.

"I'd guess it were some sort of mold or fungus," I continued. "Who knows these days," Michael offered, "With the odd weather we've been having I wouldn't be surprised if we had unusual blooms." The weather had been odd, with dramatic swings from curtains of snow to unbearable heat just overnight. The condensed seasonal cycle would produce a sense of watching the years fly by.

I nodded my head and continued to my vehicle. The evening drive proved arduous. Cars weaved in and out, as the radio blasted the latest round of untruths surrounding the political state. Fraud. Conspiracy. Lies. Scandal. The absurdity of misinformation plastered our brains as headlines shouted contradictions of themselves. As an engineer and scientist, I could not understand the beliefs of the radical fringes and the newfound disdain for truth. But then what was truth anyways, but a transient axiom driving the nature of reality? These days, people bought into their reality, and the hyper-personalized internet algorithms further fed the monster of belief. I switched to a podcast.

Upon my return to my loft, I switched on the news, balancing a light addiction to the noise and chaos. It had appeared that the orange substance had caught the attention of the local news, proving that my experience prior had not been an isolated incident. The television camera moved slowly over the foothills, scanning the boulders and foliage pausing briefly to highlight the patchy tinge of orange creeping over the rocks and leaves. A prairie dog skirted the boulder's edge, with the tips of its fur on fire with the orange dust. The cause and source were unknown, and the effects of interaction are yet to be determined. Caution was advised, but only as a side note.

I logged on to my computer intending to finalize a few emails and of reviewing a presentation regarding the integrated robotic operations of spacecraft berthing. I was a systems engineer for a small aerospace company building a spacecraft to transport humans and cargo from the ISS. As I logged on, my chat window popped up and a coworker posed, "Have you seen the orange dust?" She sent a link following, and I took the bait.

The headline read, "Unusual Orange Substance Popping Up Around the World." I skimmed through the photographs from various locations on the globe. A family in Queenstown, New Zealand stood smiling in front of an orange-tinted Lake Wakatipu. In another photo, a Swedish tourist couple posed next to the feet of Christ the Redeemer, which appeared to have acquired an orange growth between the toes. Another showed a lanky man, his skin was dark and glistening. He stood in front of a mseman cart in a swarming medina, holding in his bare hand a sticky glob of orange sludge.

"What is it?" I asked my coworker.

"I don't know. They don't know. It was observed in China first. It seems to come in various forms: dust, mold, slime. All the same neon orange color."

"Weird. Is it dangerous?"

"No news on that yet."

"Any news on that thermal analysis report?"

"Ha! Yeah, Mark is still working on it. Should be done tomorrow. Are you going to watch the EVA tonight?" The astronauts at the International Space Station were scheduled to do a spacewalk or extravehicular activity.

"No," I replied.

Most of my coworkers bled space. It was their passion, and they kept up to date on all the latest news and developments. They had photographs of themselves as children holding stuffed spaceships and dressed in astronaut Halloween costumes. Most of the time their passion irked me. It felt almost like I was being mocked. Everyone felt something, some felt everything, but I felt nothing. I wished I could feel a thirst for something or even just a spark of interest. Worst yet, I felt obliged to feign their levels of enthusiasm. Not even to assimilate really, just to pass as a human being.

Space didn't so much interest me as much as challenge me. I liked the harsh environments, and that space could be both isolating and expansive all at once. It seemed to be an equalizer. I liked that there was still so much to learn. But it was by no means a passion, and more of a way to busy my mind. I hoped at least it contributed to something larger, but sometimes it just felt frivolous and superfluous, as my existence.

I finished my work and logged off. I thought about reaching out to someone to grab a drink but decided against it. There was no one I wanted to talk to, and nothing I wanted to talk about. I felt stressed about politics since it was an election year and the news had already begun coverage. It was a taboo topic though since I had no idea who leaned which way. I had been shocked by the previous election's results and it rocked me and my understanding of what the country stood for. I would not make that mistake again.

I watched the news, ate dinner, did some reading, and then headed to bed. The evenings of workdays always felt measured. I counted down the hours until I could climb into bed next. But the sooner I went to sleep, the hastier the next conscious interlude would return, and I would have to face it all over again.

The next days felt the same. The morning commute, the meetings, the mindless watercooler talk, the forced smiles. Even the orange dust was still there, with holes where my footprints had been the day before. The evenings felt like reruns. My solace was the vibration of the city around me. I felt the presence of all the lives that surrounded but never touched me. It reminded me of electrons vibrating in place, held together by invisible bonds—and those bonds were all I needed to not be completely alone.

I, as well as the rest of the world, also listened in on China. Within a month's time, the news tone had shifted from novel curiosity to hesitation and back. The latest headline read, "China Reports Death Linking Respiratory Failure to Orange Mold". The picture showed an elderly Chinese man, respirator attached, frail and eyes wild. His eyes were a sickly orange hue. Directly below, an article titled "The Healing Properties of Orange" undermined the previous warning.

Chapter 3

Chapter 2:

S pring's fragrant air rolled in, and the neon dust swept in with it. The landscape was powdered with a light dusting, blurring the distinction between the sky and the ground. The mold had spread from doorsteps and foliage to the greater cityscape. But the news told me this was of no concern. Sneezing and coughing formed a familiar melody in the public streets, but the government officials reassured us. Most people went on with their lives in tragic ambiguity.

I'm not exempt from that group; in that, I did nothing to prepare. However, a moment came for me, when I no longer could deny the link between the mold and the symptoms, nor the possibility that this had spread globally. I could no longer deny the severity of the situation. That moment came when a Chinese doctor passionately pleaded with the world from his death bed to take this threat seriously. His actions were condemned by the Chinese government, but his punishment was eluded by his own demise. The sickness, glowing bright orange in his eyes, had taken control. His plea was a ringing alarm to the rest of humanity, which went mostly ignored. More cases of the disease had been discovered around the world, including in the United States.

Out of caution and perhaps a dash of misery, I did little else outside of work and keep up with the news of the infection. I also battled depression and anxiety, as all humans who are awake should. For anxiety is the dizziness of freedom, and depression the anchor of truth. When I interacted with my colleagues, I pictured them as skeletons, orange and glowing. What I'd come to realize is that most people don't consider nonexistence as an option. Their default is set at "living". I didn't know how frequently the average person considered death, but even at this time of viral unknowns, I guessed it as still a lot less than I did. My brain thought that at every moment, there is an evacuation option, an escape lever—an option to not exist any longer. So, each moment is weighed against the alternative and most of the time my assessment showed inconclusive results, or something close to a draw. But what it takes to not exist doesn't cross my mind. Just instead the unsettling internalization that living is a choice.

As I battled my inner dimness, the world had given the noxious growth a name, Emissary Orange, drawing a link between the foreign orange fungus and the respiratory issues erupting. It became a phenomenon whose scope was immeasurable and whose origins alluded detection. What was known, however, was the pest was an orange siphonophore. It grew its form in relation to the environment around it. It built limbs when needed and organs to digest the vulnerabilities of humanity. This growth reminded me of my artificial intelligence work in graduate school. I'd built robots that could recover from the loss of a limb. Defense money of course. The ultimate feat of evolution, with no waste. The growth's spores, when disturbed, formed a Fibonacci-shaped swirl midair. It spread through the air and was thought to be passed on through respiratory droplets. Like the misinformation, it preyed on all, but mostly the elderly and ill.

One evening, I decided to have a drink with my friend, Ruth, at the bar nearby. The evening was cool, and the two of us friends sat inside. The walls were deep emerald green, and the gold fixtures popped against them. A mural of a map highlighted the specialty drinks of various regions with embellished paint strokes. The seats were wide and low, and a candle sat on the middle of the table. The effects were that of sitting on the ground around a campfire but a little more opulent.

Ruth and I ordered cocktails. Ruth sat across from me and her wavy blond hair mimicked the gold curves of the chandelier. She dressed simply, but classic. You almost couldn't tell the decade based on her look. She would fit in in 1960 as well as she did today. Ruth worked as a civil rights lawyer for a local nonprofit. She was brilliant and quick, but it almost made her unrelatable, as if she were more of an aspiration than a person. She and I had met at a town hall.

"So how are you these days Cayden? It has been too long," Ruth started as the waiter returned our orders. I took my glass from the waitress and a long sip staring at Ruth. The harshness of the liquor felt particularly pungent. The shock to my body felt welcome.

"Oh, I've been fine I suppose. How are you?" I brushed off the question. I always hated being asked how I was. Did they even care? Do they want to know the truth? Are they just being polite? I had been raised to be polite above all else, so I typically provided a short but sufficient response and deflected back to others.

"I've been so busy. This current administration has been stripping rights left and right. Funding has been cut dramatically as well."

"How many cases are you working, right now?" I asked.

"I have nine major ones that I'm working, right now. We have so many." Ruth looked down at her drink then back up at me. I felt like she was more looking through me than at me. She was in her own world.

"Do you want to talk about it?"

"It's just all so unbelievable how people treat each other. But with ignorance follows greed and hatred. Let's talk of something else."

"Of course."

"So, what do you think of this Emissary Orange? Have you seen any of the orange mold in your part of town?" she asked.

"I saw some by work but that's quite a ways out. Haven't seen too much in the city but here and there."

"Are you concerned? Should we be concerned?"

"If the scientists and doctors think it's dangerous, I'm partial to agree with them."

"But conflicting reports have been coming out."

"There is so much misinformation out there it's hard to distinguish the truth. Probably better to be cautious."

"True. If it were serious, you would think the government would have stepped in by now. I shouldn't have to resort to research to get the news," said Ruth.

"You'd think. We should just stay away from it and avoid anyone who has been near it." I paused for a sip. "How is Martin? He still traveling a lot?"

"He is doing well. He flies out to D.C. for work once or twice a month, which isn't bad. His family recently visited us which was quite nice. Are you seeing anyone these days?" Ruth added.

"No, not really. Love always felt violent to me."

"Violent?"

"Construction is filled with violent tasks. You hammer, you drill, you sand, you saw. Yes, in the end, you've built a home, but it was built of violence. Of a million tiny sacrifices of your self-determination."

"Cheers," said Ruth with a shrewd smile.

"Cheers."

Chapter 4

Before long, the world had begun to understand the severity of Emissary Orange. Shadowed by political unrest, the news of the disease became tied to a partisan agenda. Divided the world became between believers and non. Conspiracy theories plagued our phones, our computers, our televisions. Perhaps the illness was a conspiracy to suppress the protests and lock people in their homes. Or perhaps it was an attack from a foreign government. Or maybe it was our own. Maybe an experiment has gone wrong. The authorities used the opportunity to further sever foreign relations by charging the Chinese for its conception.

Mixed guidance on precaution led to choice, a burden on the people of the world to determine their levels of concern. The rest of the world looked on at America and decided it was too dangerous to keep open to us their borders. The nation had once been the admiration of the world, but now instead, our allies locked their doors. Eventually, masks were recommended as a precautionary measure, and sanitation items such as hand sanitizer, toilet paper, and paper towels became in high demand. I had heard of a man who had hoarded hand sanitizer, spending over $16000 to stock up and resell. People always find a way to monetize pain.

The state enacted a mandatory shutdown in an attempt to control the spread. All non-essential businesses were to close that evening, leaving open only the grocery stores, pharmacies, and medical offices. Word came through social media that the city was to be shut down, so I rushed to pick up a few items before it the stores closed indefinitely. Of course, for me, essentials were cannabis and alcohol, and it appeared the many held the same in esteem based on the lines around the block.

As I waited in line at the dispensary, I could sense the panic of fellow customers. Most were urgent to fill their orders and return to the safety of their homes. Yet not everyone believed the words of science. The news had become so polarized that science itself had turned into a faith that one had to buy into. It made me feel like a priest preaching the words of science for a living. The man in front of me grew agitated, and it was noted by concerned eyes that he was not wearing a mask. Upon being greeted by the sales representative, the man was told that a mask was required to enter the building.

"My body, my choice", he says summoning the anthem of suppressed women around the world.

"Bullshit," murmured the woman behind him.

"Sir, masks are required for your safety and the safety of others," said the sales rep whose white name tag broadcast the letters P-E-T-E across his chest.

The man in front of him twitched with anger. He couldn't have been much older than 25. His head was shaved short, but you could see a halo of light blonde fuzz. He wore a black over-sized hooded jacket, jeans wide and slung low on his hips, and sneakers splattered with orange dust. He rubbed his nose with his hand, leaving behind a trace of orange beneath his nose. I noticed then the scar on his lip, something that looked like recovery from a cleft lip. My grandfather had had a similar procedure.

The man leaped forward, grabbing Pete by the shoulders, and tossing him to the floor. Pete, large but imbalanced, thudded to the ground knocking up the orange dust brought in by shoes and the wind. Pinning Pete below him, the man yanked off the sales representative's mask and coughed a forced, violent cough right into his mouth. He began spewing out threats, as I rushed forward to pull him off the innocent man.

Dismounted, the angered man brushed himself off and retreated to the exit flailing his arms in signal to the other non-believers. The woman knelt forward helping Pete to his feet, as I resumed my spot in line. Pete wiped his face, then circled around the counter to report the incident to the police. I could hear over the phone the muffled voice of the recipient. "We don't even know if masks do anything," said the administrator on the phone. "We cannot enforce their use." They agreed to tend to the violent attack, however. Around this time, another sales representative stepped forward and assisted me in completing my purchase.

I walked next to the liquor store. The line was even longer than at the dispensary. Restless people, both masked and bare, stood waiting for their turn to stock up. I joined the line; grateful I was able to leave work early to tend to these things. I checked my phone to pass the time. In doing so I saw a carousel of images of crowds waiting in lines across the region. People gathered in hoards at the grocery, convenience, and liquor stores. I never before had to hoard food, nor had I ever felt fear as to where my next meal would come from. Until the orange settled in, that is. It was an odd moment of reality for me, as it awakened something more primal inside. I waited, less patiently.

Only twenty minutes into the shutdown news broke that the mandates were repealed. The government clearly did not understand what locals considered essential and the chaos and lack of preparation brought up safety concerns. That wouldn't be the last time the officials negated their own advice, as the medical community and politicians battled between saving the economy and saving its people. Such fickle news was not uncommon. The crowds dissipated some, leaving many to wonder how serious this all could be.

That evening was my last night of normalcy. Or rather the night before was because the night of was divided. Some ran to bars, clinging to any last experience out of the house before the quarantine. Others stocked up and sheltered. I did the latter despite being tempted otherwise. Social media portrayed both warnings of caution and the frivolity of those looking for a last hurrah. I could hear those who chose the other route. Loud music shook the surfaces, and overlapping voices layered the air. My neighbor had thrown a party to send off the last sliver of normalcy. I raised the volume on the news.

Chapter 5

My company, as many others had done, closed its doors to in-person attendance. I was resigned to working remotely. Fringe to defense, the aerospace world had been dubbed critical work. Government contracts held strong. I had worked in the aerospace and defense industry since my undergraduate days, being sucked in by a national laboratory first. I had moved to Albuquerque to balance the weight of nuclear sanctity upon my head. I had a high-paying engineering job that involved assessing the lethality of native and foreign missiles. I told myself, upon accepting the job, that nuclear weapons needed to be kept safe, and that was what helped me sleep at night. But as time weighed on, I questioned what I was doing with my skills and what it all meant. That mixed with the anxiety and depression made life arduous and fevering.

I felt trapped yet burdened by freedom. I was empty but heavy. Time twisted and fluctuated, making the days feel both too long and short concurrently. There was no past or future, but instead, only regret and fear. Everything felt mundane or menacing, or both. Nothing and everything mattered, and I was being torn apart. I wanted only to feel something other than the veiled numbness of a frozen soul.

Eventually, I had quit that job. It was truly a last-ditch attempt at subduing the pain of existing. I would do whatever I believed would make me happy, because if that couldn't do it, I had no other resort. No contingency plans. So, I traveled for a year. Starting in Brazil, I migrated to Argentina and then wintered in Morocco. In Brazil, I learned the true flavors of fruit and the kindness of young strangers. Argentina taught me how small the world could truly be, and Morocco taught me restraint.

From there, I took a boat from Africa to Europe, landing in Spain first. I began to realize running doesn't affect change. I returned home to see to my Father's surgery but returned to Europe by way of Croatia. There I realized that death could take one of my own. From Croatia, east I went to Montenegro, Romania, Bosnia & Herzegovina. I learned about boundaries and beliefs. Having grown tired, I retreated to Germany then returned to the United States to settle in Denver. I had always loved Berlin, but now that this time it was familiar, it felt used. I spent my year in search of meaning and found only that I must define it myself. I had left behind everything that I had known to start over. I gave myself to the world, and it had nothing for me. I volunteered, I made relationships, and I held nothing for my own. "What did you do with all of your time?", they asked upon my return to the United States. "How was it?". But I felt dismayed by these questions. My time traveling filled a lifelong dream, and now I had no more. The journey had not filled my void, but instead echoed the emptiness of it. In response, I settled into a cozy 9-80 schedule and tried to find meaning in expanding the understanding of space and its great unknowns.

I rose at 6 A.M. to start my first day of remote work. It felt like a sick day or a holiday in some ways. I stayed in pajamas until the next day, feeling the contrast of the coziness it provided against the harsh, cold work demeanor. Being a defense company, video calls were banned, and therefore, it was completely acceptable to roll out of bed and start work without hesitation or a comb. I was reminded of all those people who were out of a job due to the shutdown and quarantine. I hoped it wouldn't last long, as the media and government had been describing.

"Are you working remotely today?" I asked a coworker.

"No. The manufacturing group had been considered critical, and therefore we must come in," Tristan responded. "My wife had to take leave from work to watch the children since schools are closed."

"Officials keep pushing to open schools, despite the safety issues. Kids need normal they say."

"Kids need to be kept safe," Tristan retorted.

After work, I took the pedestrian bridge over the railroad tracks to the grocery store to obtain a stockpile of necessities. My neighbor, Sophie, had joined me. The two of us walked with wavering distance balancing the desire to be heard with the safety of space. We avoided the patches of tangerine on the ground. Denver was a clean city, but since the growth, it had assumed an orange afterglow. We entered the store through the parking garage, grabbed a cart with hesitation, and entered the building. The store was empty, minus a few other stragglers who had not prepared for their quarantine. The last remaining products littered the floor and dotted shelves.

Sophie and I looked at one another for comfort. No canned goods, no pasta, no paper products, no cleaner. The frozen food aisles held a little relief though, as Sophie was vegetarian and most of that food was overlooked.

"If the government didn't subsidize meat so much, they'd have a real chance", Sophie commented as she picked out frozen dinners for one.

That day, Sophie had showered for the first time in a week. She stepped out of the shower and wiped off the mirror with her towel. She observed herself for a mere moment before covering her body and proceeded to comb her wet, heavy hair. The music from her living room had been quieter over there, but Sophie could still make out the melody. She hummed along gently as she made her way into the bedroom, hesitating as she approached her clothes on the bed. She had stared down at the black undergarments, the grey wool sweater, and the buttery black leggings. Sophie dreaded clothing. When she wore clothing, her body felt like a trash bag filled with live snakes. They roll over each other, stretching the limits of the bag. They made her aware of parts of her body that she never focused on before. She fantasized about slicing into her body and carving out the real one inside of that she knew was there. Instead, she had finished drying her body and donned the outfit. She was strong and independent, but only because she'd been disappointed. Sophie had been raised to believe she could achieve anything and it all, leaving her perpetually dissatisfied. But she was intelligent and beautiful despite her hauntings. She was lean if not thin, with long black hair that shone indigo.

Sophie's skin was fair and her eyes dark. "Like chocolate", her father had said. "Like shit," her younger brother would quip.

Clothed and clean, Sophie sat down at the kitchen table. She turned on the news as she did too often and pulled open her laptop to search for a new occupation. She had been unemployed all month, having lost her job as a waitress. The owners had decided to retire early due to the restrictions and the lack of customers. The bar had laid off its staff, so every day she searched. She reached out to acquaintances for help, for she didn't have many close friends. She did have her boyfriend though. She'd found the man who disappointed her the least and made him hers.

Floating through classifieds, Sophie couldn't help but notice all the advertisements for Sweepers. Her cat joined her on the couch when she heard a knock at the door. It was Cayden, curious as to whether she was interested in making the mecca to the grocery store.

Sophie finished stocking her cart with a meager two meals and a bottle of bleach, and they continued to the next aisle. Food and paper products would not be restocked for a month. The two of us purchased our items and returned home. That would be the last time we saw one another.

The weeks turned into months. None of it seemed real to me. Hundreds of thousands of people were reported to be infected. Tens of thousands dead. Each new milestone on the counter is compared to other atrocities, such as war, depression, or disease. Yet many still were consumed with disbelief. A straight rejection of the science and of journalism and public policy. The streets were covered in the orange dust, it stirred in the air and multiplied. Leaf blowers were used to clear the streets, and fire hydrants were used to scrape it off the buildings. Yet some remained unconcerned, convinced that this display was that of extremist making.

Rumors spiraled about the neon powder that it could even have medicinal purposes. Miscommunication and theories are bred in the dark parts of the world, surfacing in all forms of media. The people looked to their leadership for guidance, but the leadership was broken. Local officials sparred with federal employees to manage the spread. Instead of a federal plan to combat the effects, federal leadership leaned on state officials to come up with a plan. Therefore, each state varied in its approach.

I was precautious but also enjoyed the excuse to be alone. So, I isolated and watched the news which took up the matter and inquired as to whether our government was doing enough. Or was it doing too much? It depended on who you asked. But I wondered that day whether reporters were even allowed to tell the truth anymore.

One truth, though, was that government realized the importance of having proper lower-level employment to maintain the economic prosperity of the elite few. Therefore, the authority, teaming with some of the largest monsters in tech, created a new application in lieu of direct monetary relief. Since the orange dust had come, the demand for someone to come and clean it off their homes and their cars skyrocketed. There was now a new app to match Sweepers with customers, banking on the gig economy of the time. It was a dangerous and ill-paid occupation, but for many, it was all that was available.

Chapter 6

There was hope that the warmer weather and heat would kill off the Emissary Orange, but there was no clear proof behind that. And when summer came, the Denver sun melted the light orange snow, creating pools of glittering gold. By this time, I had been working remotely for months and had lost all sense of boundary. Bounds of time, bounds of place, bounds of the mind all began to fall away.

Emissary Orange had become a part of our everyday lives, though the deaths did not. I didn't know anyone personally who had caught it, but there had been three confirmed cases at work, a few via acquaintance, and my friend, Evie, was a nurse. I remembered also the orange mold Michael and I had seen months ago, out in the office parking lot—my first interaction with the suspected Emissary Orange. But death is of no substance without seeing demise. Or perhaps it was the human incapacity to comprehend such large numbers of deaths.

Despite this, I still trusted truth would prevail. I knew not that one cannot depend on the truths of others. One must realize that no knowledge is certain and any meaning we may bring to it is of our own doing. The warmth, did though, seem to create an oasis from the sickness and people once again began leaving their homes.

Until then, I spent my days fighting away a nagging feeling of nothingness. With nowhere to go, and nothing to do but wander the empty streets of downtown and the park adjacently so. I covered the same streets miles and miles over. Having lived in Denver for three years, it had been enough time for me to really understand the traces of the city. And with time it began to feel small and sanitized. I felt the need to sleep the days away, to numb my thoughts, and to quiet my body. I puzzled, I painted, I read, I wrote, I watched, I paced, but mainly I avoided—avoided Emissary Orange. Yet still, I was burdened by choice. I understood that I was constantly being forced to push against and upward to fight off the consequences of freedom. The meaning of that didn't originate but was chosen by me in my actions.

But now things seemed to be rounding the corner, with the disease at least. I began going back into the office once a week to feel what that felt like again. I showered for those days, donned myself with scratchy professional clothing, and felt relieved by a reason to leave my house. The roads were empty as I drove toward work, the landscape transitioning with a hump in the road from suburbia to the grandeur of the flatirons. On the highway, I unknowingly passed a semi-truck filled with Emissary Orange victims.

Sophie, on the other hand, was left unemployed and overspent. She spent her days searching for jobs and entertaining her feline, Lauren. Each day had been reduced to excruciating intervals between too delicate of meals; hunger had set in. The news reports credited the warm weather with the declining number of cases and the decreased mass of Emissary Orange. Yet only the stock market was showing economic recovery. Her current situation left her alone with her thoughts, a dangerous companion. She began questioning herself and her life in ways she had never done so before. She thought about how sometimes she would lie just to see if anyone would notice the inconsistencies. Her boyfriend usually didn't.

She asked herself, "When did boredom come into existence?" She imagined that at some point activities found basic now were once requisite of neurons firing at full capacity. It left no resources to allocate toward the vacancy of boredom.

She felt she could be diabolical but didn't care for preying on the weak. She was the kind of person who dreamed vaguely. She pictured an idyllic moment around a campfire in the mountains with friends. However, she never visualized the friends she actually had. She instead leaves them vague and ill-defined, like all her real relationships these days.

With these thoughts spinning in her head, she stared outside her window. Orange dusted the windowsill outside, and those of her neighbors. Someone had swept the sidewalk to clear a path. Sophie was tired of being impoverished and afraid. She had no clear guidance on how to stay safe from the disease besides hiding. And hiding unleashed her head.

She had sought professional help over the last decade, resulting in a variety of diagnoses. Some thought her not sick enough to treat, while others wanted to sedate her with medication to replace the pain with numbness. She felt that she was splitting apart. The vulnerabilities and shame were separated from her external life and dwelled inside her screaming to be let out. Meanwhile, her external self was composed and functional. It felt like lying. She was drowning, flailing her arms for help, while onlookers thought she was merely waving a greeting.

Most of the time she felt as if she was dissociated from her own body as if she were an outsider watching herself. Her body became a puppet with only bare threads holding together her self and her robotic gestures. She felt completely alone at a table of friends. Sophie felt nothing for them. But sometimes her inner psyche burst out into the world. Emotions would over-whelm her and almost materialize externally. It was never joy, but instead anger, frustration, or sorrow. It was unbearable. So, she did what she could about it. She opened the cabinet below her sink, pulled out the bleach, and poured herself a glass.

Chapter 7

There should have been a funeral for Sophie, but civil unrest settled in. Another death, across the country, had overtaken the broadcast. The systemic racism of U.S. institutions was being put on display in the streets using leftover craft materials. A black man had been killed by the police, suffocated. Justice was in demand and police reform was coveted. On the day of the first protest, I had followed the story on the news. People were taking to the streets despite the health concerns, risking their lives for the cause. They fought for equality when they could have sought revenge. I thought momentarily to invite my neighbor to join me on the streets, but it passed as reality phased in.

I logged off my computer, grabbed my mask, and closed the door behind me as I entered the hall. Sophie's cat slinked out of the shadowed corner and meowed at me. I stroked the cat's back, and it nuzzled its head against my hand. I promised to get food for it later. I made my way down the angular spiral staircase and pushed out the door. My residence was in Capital Hill, so it was no far walk to find the others. Walking north on Pearl St, I noticed the auburn shadows of the cottonwood leaves bouncing atop the orange brushed sidewalk. The buildings on either side of me—old but loved, displayed wide front porches, angular roofs, pillars, and vines.

Turning on 13th, I could see fellow dissenters taking to the street in demonstration. Signs bobbed in the ocean of masked people, arms were raised, and chants collided in the air above. The crowd was like blood moving through veins in the heart of the city. It throbbed more than marched due to the sheer size. Similar demonstrations lit up cities and towns around the world. For the first time in ages, a feeling swept over me. It was crushing and dense. I felt justified, less alone, and a little saner. I pulled out my phone, texting my coworker, Mason, to see if he was buried somewhere deep in the crowd. He was indeed, and we marked a place to meet. I headed toward the Denver Post building and there I found Mason. Mason was a buoyant soul who brought levity to each of his interactions. His optimism provided a striking contrast to my own attitude, but the two of us balanced each other well. I grounded Mason's lofty hopes, and Mason's levity lightened my load. We tapped elbows in replacement of a handshake and exchanged greetings.

"Cayden, how are you? Are you holding up these days?", inquired Mason, adjusting his mask such that it properly covered his nose.

"I'm hanging in there. The days have begun to blur together, and I've managed to devalue the tracking of time. I've been quarantining and have been losing myself to conversations in my head," I replied. "How are you?"

"I've been doing well. I've focused my energies on creation and exercise. I've found the slower pace to be refreshing, but I can understand your plight," offered Mason.

"Time! Such a burden of choice," I followed. Mason smiled behind his mask, but I could still recognize it in his eyes.

We joined the crowd, weaving in and out of the fellow protestors. The overall atmosphere was that of compassion, minus a few outliers. A man in a wheelchair was stuck by the curb, and before I could respond, three others donned in all black rushed to assist.

Contrasting comradery was the shadowing of militant forces creeping in at the edges of the demonstration. Heavily armed officers and military men lined the boundaries of the streets, clogging the arteries of the movement. The men were dressed in gear fit for a war—helmets, bulletproof vests, batons, guns, shields, tear gas, and tasers. Several of these men moved toward Mason and Cayden, as if marching. Some of the crowd began to fall away but others remained, steadfast in their stance. The armed men lurched forward forcing people to give way around, between, and below them. An elderly man was toppled in the wake, his frail, stiff body tipping backward. His head knocked the ground and his glasses bounced off his nose. There was blood.

I've had a complicated relationship with the police, for a particular encounter had forever stained my view of law enforcement. I had been living in Milwaukee completing my undergraduate degree in Mechanical Engineering. It was Halloween and Water Street was packed with fantastical characters. The sidewalks were crowded, and excitement vibrated through the rambling mass. It was close to midnight, and I was meeting friends at a bar nearby.

I paused between parked cars, looking for a clearing in the road to cross. I found an opportunity and proceeded into the street. Halfway across the street, I was approached by a man in uniform. The man almost seemed like a caricature of law enforcement, and I couldn't tell if it was a costume or an official. He had a thick mustache, a stiff gait, and a stern expression.

"Police. Come with me," said the officer, and I followed him to the sidewalk. The officer questioned me on my drinking that night and my rationale for jaywalking. I had had a few drinks, but nothing extensive. The officer didn't seem to believe this.

"Do exactly as I do," the officer said firmly.

Officer Mitchell scratched his nose briefly, then stepped forward with his right leg. He placed each foot in front of the other, heel to toe. He took 15 steps, turned 180 degrees to his left, and walked back.

"Now you," said Mitchell.

I followed suit. I stepped forward with my right leg, walked the 15 paces, turned left, and returned to the officer. I looked to the officer for confirmation of completion.

"You didn't scratch your nose. You failed."

The officer was aggressive and shackled me without regard for my broken finger. I had broken it a few weeks before. Pain shot up through my hand and up my arm. My doctor had told me to keep the finger elevated, but my hands were bound low behind my back and the handcuffs had cut off circulation to my hand completely. I told the officer of my injury and he told me I should have thought of that before I broke the law. I was being taken in on account of jaywalking and public intoxication.

I waited handcuffed, plopped on the curb for three hours while the officer tagged others for similar offenses. By that time, the streets had emptied but for a few stragglers, and the bars had been closed for over an hour. Neon lights hummed in the distance. The officer arrested a witch, a Roman emperor, and a vampire in total. With the approach of a police van, Mitchell summoned us, delinquents, to our feet. The van stopped in front of us, and Mitchell swung open the two back doors to the van. The officer put his hand on each of our heads, pushing forcefully downward as we entered the vehicle one by one.

In the darkness of the van, the witch began to cry. It was hard to see it, for it was dim and her face was painted a silvery green, but I could hear it. I could see her visibly quivering. Her pointed hat bent at an odd angle, straining to fit under the low roof. The van started and jolted forward, causing those of us handcuffed in the back to bounce and fall into one another. There was no seatbelt, not that we could put one on themselves. The witch sprung upward with the bump further crushing the dark velvet of her hat. She landed on the edge of the bench but slid off it thumping to the ground. She remained there in defeat.

"Are you okay?" I asked. I adjusted in my seat.

"Is anything okay?" she retorted.

"Good point," quipped the emperor.

The crew remained silent for the rest of the ride. After twenty minutes or so, the van parked, and the offenders were escorted into the police station. The group was split into male and female, and the officers lined them up for photos and patdowns.

I was patted down first, and I made eye contact with the witch as she was subjected to the same dehumanizing activity. She looked concerned. The female officer started by patting her arms and made her way to the witch's torso. The officer paused, looking up inquisitively at the sorceress. The green witch smiled nervously. The officer resumed her search making her way down the legs and toward the crotch.

"What the…?!" exclaimed the female officer.

"I'm trans," the witch replied quietly.

"Get over there!" the officer shouted pointing at the line where I stood.

"But I'm not—"

"GO."

I was escorted to a changing room and was given an orange jumpsuit to don. My personal items were taken and bagged. I was ushered to a cell and locked in for the night.

Chapter 8

had become obsessed with watching the news. If I wasn't checking it on my phone, I was watching it on television or searching through online articles between breaks at work. I balanced my news consumption between the two opposing views that existed and divided the country: *the Abstract* and *the Tactile*. Or at least it used to be two. The country had fractured from just two major parties and new factions popped up daily that further tightened the fragile thread holding the country together. Now people fought over graduated views within these domains, and further, fought on individual issues. Gun rights, abortion, funding, health care, unemployment, marriage rights, equality.

I, at present, flipped through all the stations to understand what I could from all perspectives, since none could longer be trusted.

"Emissary Orange has hit us with a second wave. Cases are again increasing," said the news anchor. The heat has not killed the growth as many had hoped."

Next.

"Good evening, this is Gail Henderson with Channel 7 news. We come to you today with breaking news on the protests happening all around the country. Black Lives Matter or BLM protests have sprung up in cities across the world, lending a voice to those who haven't been heard. But what about the opposition? Tonight, we will be talking about the protests to the protests. First up are the white supremacist marches in the South. Tiki torch-wielding men in white, both hooded and not, marched down the streets tonight. A large cross had been set aflame in the town center. We take a look now—"

I changed the channel.

"Joining us today is the father of the man suffocated by the police. He expresses his pain at the lack of charges against the police officers involved. No justice has been served and he—"

Next.

"Thank you for joining us, Karen and Chad." The news anchor looked back at the camera, "With us here is the couple who pulled out rifles to greet the BLM protestors passing their property in downtown St. Louis. Were they within their rights?"

Next.

"We are tired of hearing about Emissary Orange," started a woman dressed in a light blue dress and heels. "Can't we get on with our lives? Let's talk about something else already! I'm trying to live my life."

Next.

"Do not be alarmed! We have Emissary Orange totally under control. Totally. We couldn't have it better under control. You ask the people—you know the people—if we could just— The orange dusting—you know it's more of glow isn't it? It's harmless. I even think it might be good for you. The experts—," touted the Authority.

Next.

"Do you really know the Abstract authoritarian candidate? Stay tuned for his connections to the Illuminati, Communism, and the sex scandal that will rock the—"

Next.

"Hospitals across the country are concerned about the number of patients being admitted to the hospital for Emissary Orange. Hospital beds are in high demand, patient care has been moderated, and logistics of body removal have yet to be determined. Lines form—"

Next.

"—the Authority did, in fact, know about the severity of the Emissary Orange, but downplayed it because, and I quote, "The public mustn't be alarmed.""

Next.

"Hundreds gather to celebrate ignoring the guidelines of our health officials. We join you now live from—"

I turned off the television. Somehow, the city was still surprised at each new outbreak. It seemed out of place under the beautiful blue Colorado skies. But stupidity had an aptitude for getting its way. People had forgotten to be modest and thought they could live their lives as usual, while America was running a temperature. The growth had returned at full force.

Chapter 9

By this time, 638,169 people had died from Emissary Orange across the world. There were 8,982,020 confirmed cases of Emissary Orange. Five percent of those tested, which were not many due to the lack of preparation, tested positive for the disease. It could spread asymptomatically. The Center for Disease control was providing untethered guidance to wear masks in public. For the first time, the Authority wore a mask in public. Yet his goal was not to educate but belittle. He wore the mask in mockery of his electoral opponent.

To add to the misfortune, a cherished hero of the underdog has passed to natural causes, and now a vacancy in the judicial court hung on the minds of both the people and officials. The judge had been a champion of women's rights and changed the way the law saw gender. The renowned Supreme Court Judge and champion of women's rights had passed today at the age of 87.

To add further insult, the judge's replacement was to be chosen by the slanted Authority, and the woman chosen was not a shadow of her being. The replacement was a Christian and made sure you knew so. Her ideals opposed that of her antecedent, and her appointment was a step toward destabilization of the delicate balance of the court. She was a fundamentalist, a textualist. She understood nothing beyond the direct language of the constitution. She checked the box of woman but was devoid of any other clear resolution. Women around the world stood in fear of what she might do. Would she stand with them and champion them in their plight? There was already had an accused rapist on the bench. How much worse could it get?

Instead of being formed authentically and in the spirit of freedom and anxiety, it seemed to me the values of the masses were just accepted by others because that is what everyone does. Some women didn't even fight for the rights of their own bodies. The myths and media imprinted human consciousness, often to the disservice of the women. They had fallen prey to masculine sadism. The world had forgotten that one cannot assume freedom in isolation from the freedom of others. Individual freedom is interwoven with that of others by way of the world. But for some women, it was easier to assume the role of an object than to take responsibility.

Furthermore, the Authority had continued claiming that the health coverage guaranteed by the affordable care act was unconstitutional. The act provided health care for millions of Americans and protected them from preexisting conditions. The new judge, appointed by the Authority, refused to state a position on the argument leading many to believe she would follow his whims. If repealed, millions of Americans would be without health insurance during a pandemic.

The new judge's religious devotion inspired some and frightened others, for her nomination was used as an attempt to secure the evangelist vote. And perhaps to swing the court in the Authority's favor were the election results to be reviewed by the Supreme Court. The judge had been part of an authoritarian, charismatic religious group that labeled men as 'leads' and women as 'handmaids' and harkened a gender hierarchy where women should defer to men. The followers secured a covenant with God to obey the direction of the holy spirit.

I had been raised Catholic. I understood what it meant to mature in a world of heaven and hell. It was a place where devils and demons nipped at our heels, and angels hung in the sky trumpeting the soundtrack. It was a universe where you could be punished just for your thoughts, for the Lord could hear all. While honorable in their goals, organized religion, to me, seemed never to get past its own demons.

"...Lead us not into temptation," I would pronounce, in sync with my fellow students, "but deliver us from evil. For thine is the kingdom, the power, and the glory, for ever and ever." Words chanted by humans around the globe. The same oral motions, the same gusts of breath, the same vibrations echoing forth, tribal. Perhaps creatures did the same, but man could not distinguish.

I went to Catholic school for most of my childhood. I was taught by nuns, both kind and stern. They dressed in all black with accents of white around the collars. I remembered distinctly, being in that classroom kneeling in prayer. Born with the shame of original sin, my younger self felt the burden of Catholic guilt. Such weight on such tiny shoulders.

I realized that faith must be individual. Since most people were born into a religion, they do not have faith so much as a sense of community identity. They get lost in the label. I did not believe in the power of passion, as it was a devastating torrent that inevitably controls man to the commitment of certain acts. It was instead an excuse. The religious believed man could find refuge in some given sign that will guide him on earth, but I believed man interpreted signs as he pleased, and man was condemned at all time to invent man. It was not God who gave man meaning, but man. Value was not bequeathed but born. To aim at the infinite is to aim to lose sight of the self, and perfection of religion leaves no space for man.

"Amen."

I was seven years old, in-classroom mass, and needed to use the restroom. I used my hand to steady myself as I rose from my knees. I straightened my uniform. The priest noticed this movement and watched me as I silently made my way toward. The priest accompanied me to the lavatory, and hovered over me as I relieved myself.

"Thwack." A belt snapped on my lower back. I straightened.

"Faster. You are taking too long."

"Thwack," hitting my shoulder blade this time.

I finished as I could, dripping piss down the side of my leg.

Next to take the streets would be the women.

Chapter 10

It seemed that these days the world was crumbling. Megafires ravished the west, hurricanes sanitized the south, and record-breaking weather moved in. Voices on the radio were angry and confused. Once the lines of reality and belief had become blurred, violence began to dominate. Listlessness weighed heavy, as the smoke and orange ash. It felt so close yet so far. While unwise to jump to conclusions, I felt as if the world were falling out from below me. My fear had become conscious of itself and turned to anguish. All the while, the authorities waited by the sidelines to watch it all meet its natural death.

I needed human warmth. It had been months since I'd touched another human being. Being of my lonesome, I enjoyed my space. Yet the space in time grew too large. With the curfews and the limited capacities and reservations required, all pleasantries of drinking or dining out fell away. It became cold, pre-coordinated outings and events as spontaneity itself succumbed to the ashen orange. I was too cautious to meet strangers.

I've had lovers, but it never seemed to catch. Like pieces of silk sliding over each other. My problem with relationships was the dependence upon a loved one for meaning in life. It tempts one to relinquish one's freedom or tries to rob others of theirs. I instead tried to free myself from absolute devotion, and with generosity and acceptance, sought a deeper awareness of the world and the lovers themselves. I wanted to transcend together into the future while enriching ourselves and the world around us. I reached out to an old lover, Evie, to gauge interest in meeting up.

Evie engaged. She too was feeling the weight of loneliness and the ghosts of relationships passed. Both felt that the risk was worth the reward. So many had ignored the heeds of the medical experts and continued their lives with the force of habit gaining the day. It was much less risky than that, but still a risk. Evie was an ER nurse and had been working extensive hours to meet the demand of the ruthless disease. When she finished her shift that night, she saw the text and couldn't resist the opportunity. She showered and headed my way. The nurse was also the daughter of immigrants. Her parents took the treacherous journey from Mexico to Colorado before she had been born. She knew well the story of their journey. She, like her parents, believed strongly in American potential. She bought into the sentiment that productivity and efficiency could save her.

"Evie. Tell me, how are you? Did you just finish your shift?" I warmed.

She embraced me tightly and I did the same.

"Yes, I'm fine. Let's sit. We've much catching up to do," stated Evie, as she brushed her thick dark hair out of her eyes.

I poured us each a glass of wine and met Evie on the couch.

"Cayden, this is horrible," Evie started, "So much death. So much lost. The people come pouring in, dusted in orange, eyes bright and yielding. They wheeze and cough. There aren't enough people to help, there aren't enough rooms or beds, and we have no personal protective equipment. I've made a gown for myself out of a trash bag and made a mask out of an old t-shirt. And the bodies! So many bodies and nowhere to put them."

Evie mentally reviewed the last few months in her mind. She remembered distinctly a young girl and her mother in the emergency room. Evie had stood with the mother as she moved away the plastic curtain partition to reveal her daughter's plight. The girl's eyes glowed orange with swirls of red veins popping. The rest of her face was covered with respirator equipment. She wheezed and coughed violently, shaking the flexible tubing connecting the girl to the machine. The girl was pale and weak, with a sweaty fever. The mother fell to the ground crying. Her hazmat suite, required for in-person visits, made sharp popping sounds as she crumbled. She reached for Evie's leg and held on tight, crying her for daughter. The mother rushed out a string of useless prayers, promises, and tears.

"And yet some still don't believe. Any news on a vaccine?"

"No news yet. We can only treat the symptoms so far. They are trying though."

"My goodness." I shook my head.

"Worse yet, the Authority is claiming that the rise in Emissary Orange is our fault. That doctors and nurses are skewing the results for compensation benefits. It is thankless." On top of all that, she was paid less than her male colleagues.

"And dangerous," I noted.

"Not as dangerous as in Mexico," she retorted, remembering the horror stories of her parents' lives. She thought of all the families separated at the border by the United States government. Children caged and herded, parents shaking with grief.

"We also had patients in from the protest today. An SUV ran through a crowd of BLM demonstrators in its own form of protest. One dead, three injured."

"And no one charged?"

"No one charged."

"Later a woman barged in the hospital demanding we should show her the bodies, in an attempt to expose us as a conspiracy theory. She was hysterical and we had to call security." As the Emissary Cases regained momentum, so did mistrust. Since government officials and scientists were divided, the nation was too.

"All of this is so surreal," I offered, "Everything I thought this country stood for is crumbling before my eyes. Freedom, democracy, honor, leadership, equality, and excellence have been replaced with fear, division, control, and arrogance. The United States has pulled away from its allies, arrogantly thinking the country could rule in a vacuum. It feels like a dictatorship."

"I used to look at other countries and pity the corruption," Evie said despondently.

"I used to teach English to a young musician in Casablanca. He was a political activist, writing and performing rap songs on the street in opposition to the King. It was against the law to speak out against him, but he did it anyway. One day he didn't show up again for class. The other students had informed me it was likely he had been kidnapped and imprisoned. I never saw him again."

"I can't believe things like that still happen."

"I fear that is where we are headed." I leaned back in contemplation.

"Where my family is from, in Mexico, the politicians were wrapped around the fingers of the cartels and gangs. Officials turned a blind eye to the violence and murder in order to get a cut of the profits. They grew calloused to the slaying, rape, and desecration. It's still like this, which is why I send money back to my family still suffering there."

I reached for her hand and squeezed it hard.

"I'm frightened," she said. "I cannot handle another four years. The world cannot handle another four years."

Evie reached out and held my hand. I felt a rush through my body. I thought holding hands to be one of the most intimate of gestures. Its beauty lied in the repurposing of something so practical to that of novelty. Once defined by utility, these hands now were used for tenderness. Evie's hand felt small in mine. "I'm sorry," I whispered softly. I was sorry for her plight and how the tragedies of the year disproportionally affected her.

Being a white man, I understood my privilege. I'd never experienced sexual assault, never felt afraid to walk alone at night. I had never been told to go back to my country, or that my people were job-stealing rapists. I never had to teach my children of the harsh realities of racism. People weren't surprised by my education or eloquence, and I had not once been monitored or followed in a store due to my skin tone. I was never called a terrorist or had to fight for equal pay. I was able to walk the earth unaware of myself.

Evie leaned in and kissed me.

Chapter 11

While the populace was distracted by alternate truths, unemployment, and the viral strain, lead bureaucrats had begun to be systematically replaced by the Authority. Anyone who disagreed with the Authority's motives was at risk. Therefore, many stood silent. Those that didn't were replaced by more agreeable sorts. Hundreds of judges were appointed while the people were distracted.

The Authority appointed a radiologist as the head public health official for Emissary Orange. He appointed an oil and gas CEO as the head of the EPA. He set his son-in-law, a real estate broker, as head of peacekeeping in the Middle East. His head of education suggested the use of guns in classrooms to deter bears. The Authority himself was a compulsive liar. His reality was as his ego, reliant on the dishonest notion that we individually exist.

Many were attracted to the current Authority based on party lines. Others thought him to be more religious than the opponent, despite his behavior. Abortion was at the front lines of many people's concerns, and the Authority was an avid opponent to the procedure. Many believed the promises of a speedy economic recovery, and others just didn't want to be taxed more.

Some believed that America should focus inward on itself in place of providing global succor.

And there were those fascinated with the man himself. He claimed to be a self-made man, although he had inherited his wealth. He possessed businesses and buildings and millions of dollars in debt. He ignored climate change, which resonated with those in the oil and gas industry. Yet many still believed that he was the change that the United States needed. A change from the standard corrupt politician who was out of touch with the needs of their constituents. They nominated him, as a businessman, to drain the swamp. His main weapon was deploying tens of lawyers to drag on the process of persecution. The man believed he could shoot someone in public and still not lose votes.

An Authoritarian debate was held between the two parties—the incumbent Abstract and the Tactile—, and I watched in fear. I had invited over a couple of friends to watch with me. The first to join were Simon and Lua. Simon was a salesman, through and through. In his career, he had sold hospice, pharmaceuticals, and cannabis products. He made it to Denver by way of his childhood home of rural Missouri and a long intermission around New Mexico. He had sandy blonde hair, bleached naturally by extensive time in the Colorado sun. His eyes were a sharp blue, which still stood out beyond the red branches of veins covering the whites of his eyes. He was tattooed such that professional attire would cover the art. He was covered in skeletons mostly.

Lua was a manager at a liquor distribution center. She was tall and lean, with beachy light brown hair. She seemed to fade away in the background when with her boyfriend. Between the two of them, they free had access to all major events happening in the state and they took full advantage of that. I would occasionally join them on their wild adventures, but often just couldn't keep up.

We exchanged greetings, and Simon pulled out of his jacket a small bag of white powder. He smiled and walked over to the kitchen counter. Simon poured some of the contents onto the table and used his credit card to form three lines. He extracted a twenty-dollar bill from his wallet, rolled it into a tube, and snorted his line. Lua and I followed suit.

"Here we go!" shouted Simon.

A knock on the door. John had arrived. John opened the door slowly entering the living room. John was tall with chestnut skin and dark hair wound into tight curls. He was a schoolteacher, and his demeanor was made for the role.

The group paused to watch as the men took the stage. The incumbent was overweight with skin tinted orange to cover up the paleness of old age. His hair was thin and wispy, almost a ghost of itself. He smirked with his eyes squinted. His opponent, Tactile representation, appeared worn and a little sleepy. The debate kicked off with the topics of Emissary Orange and transitioned to the Supreme Court, the economy, racism, and election integrity.

Throughout the debate, the incumbent Authority could not keep silent. His words overlapped his opponents and he made childish faces at statements he thought disagreeable. He refused to answer any questions, instead, he touted vague promises of a booming economy and a great America. "Law and Order" was his latest tagline, yet the Authority did nothing to condemn violence in his name. When asked about his thoughts on rightwing extremist groups, he looked into the camera and told them to "Stand back and stand by."

The group looked inward at each other, our gazes wide and concerned.

"Did he just….?" Started John.

"Yes, he did," Lua replied.

"That sounded like a call to action," said John. "As if it wasn't hard enough being a gay black man in this society."

John had experienced enough discrimination as is. He remembered having been forced to live in bad faith by hiding his true self. In some ways that was easier. What he couldn't mask though was the color of his skin. It was even more noticeable in a place like Colorado given the substantial white majority. He watched the democratic opponent listen in disbelief at the Authority's crazed speech.

"Surely this would be enough to damn the Authority…Yet the Authority's statements about grabbing women by the pussy did nothing to deter his initial election," I speculated. The Authority had been accused of rape multiple times, yet since rape is difficult to prove, he had yet to be charged. This was the leader of the free world. I thought of the women who had voted for him in the past. I could not understand such lack of self-respect to not denounce such actions that could harm them.

"Show us your tax returns!" Simon bellowed. The Authority had refused to do so, but leaked reports showed he paid only $750 in taxes, substantially less than the average citizen. This enraged many but others felt this was merely a sign of his business savvy.

While the debate was widely considered a disaster, some news stations claimed the Authority won the debate. His disregard for precedent, tradition, and rules served him according to his followers. His supporters ignored the warning signs and blindly followed like members of a cult. Cayden feared that this may be the majority. Turning off the post-debate news coverage, Simon turned to the rest of the group scattered around the living room.

"We kind of want to try it," Simon said.

"Try what?" John asked. Moving from the kitchen island to the couch. Simon and Lua made room for him.

"Emissary Orange," Simon stated firmly.

"What the hell man? What are you talking about?" I sprung to my feet from the smoking chair. A pillow fell to the ground.

"I'm serious. Listen—" he started.

"No. This is absurd. That shit kills you. What do you think is going on in the world? People are dying!" I blurted, unfiltered.

"Yes, Simon. That is crazy talk," added John, putting his head in his hands in defeat.

"Calm down. We wouldn't breathe it in. That's what's deadly. But I heard if you lick it you get a crazy high. Lots of visual stuff," Lua offered to calm the group.

Simon and Lua exchanged glances, then looked to the group for affirmation.

"Seriously no. We don't even know what that is," John rejoined.

"It's organic obviously, like mushrooms," Simon added. "What's natural is the microbe. Everything else—health, integrity, purity—is an artifact of the sustained human will."

Days after the debate, it was announced that the Authority had contracted Emissary Orange. Since the man felt that masks were a limitation of citizens' freedom, he refused to wear one himself. However, that did not stop the infection's reckoning. Many thought this would be the reality check the country deserved, having not taken the disease seriously thus far. Meanwhile, churches sued local governments claiming capacity limitations were suppressing their religious freedom. The Authority reluctantly admitted himself to the hospital. He would spend three days there receiving world-class medical treatment including experimental drugs and steroids. After he would claim both immunity and destruction of the growth despite the increased cases. The United States had been leading the world in Emissary Orange deaths. He returned in full force pumped with steroids, claiming he had been touched by God.

In the meantime, violence continued to erupt across the country. The cult of the Abstract had begun to take matters into their own hands. In one case, an extremist group had plotted to kidnap a democratic governor claiming treason. More so, gun sales had skyrocketed. I imagined that some of those weapons would be used to enable school shootings, which occurred every few months those days. Others on protestors by people claiming self-defense. Some would be leveraged by the police to kill innocent black people. A few would be toyed with by children of gun-owning parents, resulting in injury or death. I hoped I was wrong.

Chapter 12

The election sensationalism erupted as the day of judgment drew near. The campaign rallies left behind a trail of dead and deserted. It was hard to tell how many people attended these events. In some images and videos, the crowd appeared packed and hefty, oozing with arrogance and angst. Others highlighted a sparse and meager attendance, with patches of people like moles on a back. The opposition screamed into the void but was ultimately drowned out by the absurdities of the Abstract. A Tactile tour bus had even been run off the road by trucks supporting the opposition.

The incumbent fed off the large, unmasked crowds. He was aroused by the devotion and the crowd's willingness to face death, barefaced and packed, in his honor. He obsessed over the size of the crowds and mocked his opponent for his scaledback, socially distanced rallies. He was jealous of the extensive airtime devoted to tracking the infection. He was a reality television personality before his time in office. He was vain, insecure, and childish. A dangerous combination.

The only action left was to vote. I researched each of the politicians and policies to fully understand the consequences of my choice. I knew that the results of this election would redefine

America forever. Even how close the results were would say volumes. How long would it take to get the results?

I knew that the election rules were dictated at the state level. Some could count ahead, others not until Election Day. I understood that these rules were being used as tools to restrict voter turnout. Tens of cases of voter suppression were overloading the courts with only days away. Signature matching, identification requirements, limited polling stations, fake election boxes, voter intimidation, limitations on absentee voting—all testified to the limitation of citizen access.

I decided to vote in person. I took the pedestrian bridge over the train tracks toward the conference center. I took note of the buildings, windows boarded with wood in anticipation of post-election violence. At an intersection, I waited for the light to change. I looked at the curb below staring at the orange slime pooling just below my feet.

I speculated as to how this orange goo came into existence. It had started as a dusting or powder but transformed itself independently to meet the requirements of the environment. In some places, it manifested as a slimy goop, in others, delicate ash. It had been observed bubbling and spraying. I meant to keep my distance but felt compelled to observe the foreign mass in more detail. I surveyed the ground and picked up a lengthy stick. I leaned back to provide as much distance as I could and moved the stick cautiously toward the mass. When the two made contact, it felt as the viscous form vibrated in response. I believed that everything is born without reason, that life prolongs itself out of sheer weakness and dies fortuitously. The disease would be no exception.

A sweet sickness overcame me. The world of explanation and reason was not in existence. I could not explain, classify, nor determine exactly what I was looking at. I could outline its properties, but I had created its essence. And for a moment,

I could feel the boundary between the slime and myself dissolve into a shared nothingness.

The traffic light changed, and I snapped back. I continued toward the convention center. Upon reaching the entrance, it took me twenty minutes to walk to the end of the line. Parked cars lined the sidewalks, with engines revving and exteriors plastered with propaganda. The American flag and patriotism had been appropriated to serve the Abstract. It felt like Independence Day. I joined the line, asking the man in front of me how long the wait was expected to be.

"Last I heard, we're looking at five hours," he said through his mask. The man had brought a camping chair and a cooler for the wait. He offered me a beverage.

"Bryce," he said. "Might as well get to know each other."

I didn't particularly feel like talking. I was weary of strangers. I was aloof and held a mistrust of everyone I met. I observed the people in line around me. About ten people back, there was a family with three small children. The children weaved through the crowd, screaming and yelling, throwing a red ball between them. One of the children, a small girl with blonde pigtails, dropped the ball and chased it as it rolled through piles of orange goo pushed to the side of the streets. She picked it up and continued throwing it to her brothers.

The couple behind me wielded guns. The court had recently decided that it was unconstitutional to ban firearms on election property. Also, it is unconstitutional to enforce mask-wearing, which they were not. Behind them, an elderly woman was hunched over her walking support. She looked frail and weak, and I wasn't sure how she would handle the wait. Bryce noticed as well and offered the woman his seat. She accepted.

"I'm worried," started Bryce, staring at me. "What has this world come to?"

I wavered, not knowing from where this man came. He was simply dressed, with a polo shirt and khaki shorts. He had grey hair and must have been in his 60s. He wore a mask, so he at least believed that Emissary Orange was real. But that didn't tell enough. Whose side was he on?

Bryce didn't wait for me to answer. Instead, he continued, "I worry for my family. My business is suffering from the outbreak. No customers. My daughter has a health condition, very expensive."

I still couldn't tell.

"I'm sorry to hear that," I sympathized. "What kind of business do you do?"

"I own a furniture store. What do you do?"

"I'm an engineer," I replied.

Sweepers dressed in hazmat suits, white with orange-stained limbs, passed by the line. They put their lives at risk for a minimum wage of ten dollars an hour.

In the gap of conversation, I took the moment to check my phone. I cycled through my apps mindlessly until I reached my email. I skimmed through the senders and subject lines, stopping abruptly at one marked "Your vote could cost you your life" on the subject line. I clicked to find out more.

As I scrolled through, I realized this was an Abstract extremist group threatening violence if the Authority wasn't reelected. It claimed it knew my information and it could track how I voted. I had heard news of Russia and Iran attempting to interfere in U.S. elections using such tactics. I was not swayed but was a bit uneasy. The government did nothing to deter such action, as it benefited the Authority.

Looking up from my phone, I noticed a small seemingly militant group watching from across the street. The Authority had called upon his people to go into the polls and watch very carefully. I suspected these men heard the call. Their presence was unnerving.

"Jobs, taxes, health care, foreign relations, economy, the sanctity of elections. It's all up in the air right now," continued Bryce. "All I want is the best for my family."

I agreed with the sentiment but was unsure of the man's preferred method toward resolution. I knew that wronged started by fighting for justice and ended by wanting to wear the crown. They eventually attempt to impose their individuality.

"And what about the other families?" I asked. "I think we can all agree that we want the best for our own families."

"Ah yes, and the other families of course."

"That is where the nuance lies, though," I started. "Do you want what you think is best for the families or do you want what they think is best for their families? I believe those can be very different."

"I believe in freedom, so of course the latter. I believe we need to stand up for those that cannot stand up for themselves," finished Bryce, scratching his ear.

"Agreed!" I replied, feeling more certain of the man's affiliation. He had to support the Tactile. He cared about the rights of others, of the minority who must fight for their freedom.

"Glad we're on the same page. There are some crazy abortion fanatics out there. Slaughtering babies and ripping them from the womb. It's disgusting." Bryce continued.

"Shit," I murmured. "I was talking about inequality. We need to help those who are repressed by the current system. We need to stand up for the marginalized minority."

"Oh," Bryce sighed.

We began to hear chanting in the distance. Both Bryce and I paused to listen more closely. "I am change," they shouted and echoed. I strained my neck to see around the line, witnessing a crowd moving down the street with signs. It was a small demonstration encouraging people to vote. As they moved slowly down the street, the Abstract supporters in trucks took notice. They pulled their vehicles out from their spots, blocking the street to the oncoming crowd. Soon after, the police officers noticed as well.

As the crowd drew near, I could see that the march was mainly comprised of black men. The cops shouted to halt. They hid behind their tear gas and began spraying at the group. One of the trucks sped out and ran into the crowd. I could see the bodies collapsing underneath the silver grill. The truck paused amplifying the sound of the screams. It reversed and sped out through the parking lot out onto the street. The police began handcuffing the protestors.

The line shrugged forward unphased by the scene. Someone in the crowd called 911. I stepped out of line, rushing forward to help those fallen closest to me. I helped two men to their feet. Upon rising the two men turned to help others. I stood still for a moment and absorbed the scene. The police had returned to their stations, and the rouge militant group hadn't moved.

I scanned the line meeting eyes with Bryce. He waved for me to come over. I hesitated but accepted the silent invitation stepping out of the street and onto the sidewalk. We waited four hours to cast our votes, which ultimately canceled each other out.

Chapter 13

I had a hard time focusing on my work the day of the election. I knew there would not be a result by the end of the day, but I longed for a conclusion. The news played out possible election scenarios.

"Today the Authority claimed that mail-in voting was inherently fraudulent. He claimed the ballots received after the election cannot be counted. Do not be concerned. He does not have the power to do that, and we need to believe in the integrity of our elections and democracy," Claimed Channel 7 news.

I watched the polls which had been saying that the Tactile candidate was in the lead, even in swing states. However, after the disconnect between the popular and electoral votes in the last election, I felt the polls were not to be trusted. Still, the lead was so narrow it brought no further comfort.

Furthermore, the Authority hinted at not conceding the election if he were to lose. He armed the White House like a fortress with new un-scalable fences installed around the perimeter. The man could refuse to leave. Or he could tie up the election results in legalities. And what about his supporters? I imagined riots in the streets. His supporters were already violent and aggressive in their provision.

I wondered what anger like that felt like. How did one harvest so much hate for someone they did not know? How did they claim to champion freedom when they try to oppress others based on their personal beliefs? How did they put their convenience over the lives of others in refusing to take the plague seriously? How could they put a hobby above the lives of innocent children?

Maybe it wasn't anger but desperation. Maybe they were so desperate for change that they voted for the Authority despite his character. What change were they asking for that they weren't getting from the Tactile? The rural regions faced unique disparities. Poor infrastructure, unemployment, restricted access to health care and education. A battle between the cities and the suburbs erupted, and the cities were surrounded. Cities boasted larger numbers and superior education yet were no match to the sprawling rural zeitgeist. The rural citizens had history on their side. Perhaps they didn't have the luxury to be concerned with existential threats, instead of focusing on getting through the day.

I could sympathize with that. My depression took on various filters. Sometimes it was grandiose, and I burdened myself with every plight of mankind. Every existential threat realized itself in my mind, and I felt helpless against the overwhelming weight of the world's problems.

Other times, my focus took on blinders, seeing only the absurdities right in front of me. Basic human hygiene, food consumption, and general engagement with the world around me became devastatingly burdensome. Some days I couldn't lift my head let alone get out of bed. My only hope was to make it through the day and let time heal the invisible wounds. Perhaps instead it wasn't anger but apathy that was the largest threat.

I tried to reassure myself that perhaps if the worst were to happen, at least they had a chance at the down-ballot elections.

That wasn't nearly enough. "It's progress," they might say. But I did not believe in the idea of progress. Progress implies improvement, but man remains the same. He is confronting a condition that is incessantly changing, while choice always remains a choice in any condition.

It seemed to me that a vote for the Authority was a vote to ignore the existential threats of the time. To ignore climate change, to ignore the illness, to ignore rising tensions amongst adversarial countries, to ignore a tyrannical ruler, to ignore civil unrest due to inequality. The electoral map matched that of the Emissary Orange hot spots, supporting this theory. They voted to live in ignorance and walled themselves into a rosier reality. I wondered if it would be better for man to choose depravity rather than to have good forced upon him.

The Authority continued to claim the growth was receding, as the orange dust swirled in the air around him. He touted the opposition wanted to destroy that rosy alternate reality and would destroy all their beloved holidays. He claimed his opponent would destroy the economy with his Emissary Orange mandates. He labeled the shutdown efforts a failure.

I was distracted when I called into meetings. How could I focus on building a spacecraft when something so fundamental as our basic rights was on the line? Beyond that, the future of the space program lay in the hands of the newly elected leader. Would they change the 2024 moon strategy? Would space still be a priority? Should it be a priority in these times? I often wondered if I was part of the problem rather than the solution.

While there were concrete coercions to face, some of the most menacing threats were that to the conceptual unity of the states. I thought about my own relationships and how they had been twisted by the charged political climate. Suspicion had replaced empathy. I thought of the arguments of the past holiday season. Political beliefs gerrymandered relationships, redefining the lines of acceptance. Even the closest-knit relationships were at risk. The echo chambers of social media and the press fostered bravado in expressing political standings. The divide had grown so large that we could no longer see the humanity in each other. My family, as others did, fought about the leadership of the country. In the end, we ceased talking to each other being unable to bridge the cavernous divide.

Exit polls underscored the vastly variant priorities of the Abstract and the Tactile. The major issues of the day were equality, economy, health care, and Emissary Orange. For the Abstract, equality was in last place for prioritization with only 3% of the vote. The disease was next at a mere 5%. The economy was overwhelmingly the chief priority. For the Tactile, equality was in first place at 30% and Emissary Orange followed at 22%. This provided me with some insight into the other side. As the day passed the electoral map lit up in color. The states started as red or blue but in the end, they were all orange. The real winner of this election was the growth.

Upon finishing my workday, I drifted through my apartment and found myself in the bathroom looking into the mirror. Staring at myself, I studied my face. I often studied it in these lost days, appearing as a stranger to myself. I couldn't even decide if the reflection was ugly or attractive. I felt one couldn't prescribe these qualities to it. It was like calling a boulder beautiful or ugly. I hated how expressive my face was. It proudly displayed what my heart would try to hide. Interest, joy, anger, and fear painted themselves across my features. As I looked now, I held no expression. I felt the conflicting need to understand an empty mirror and the desire to better define myself.

Looking into my own pupils was as if I was staring at the asphalt. Flat, hard, and surface. I had thick dark eyebrows which crawled above my eyes. Stubble sprinkled my chin and cheeks, for I hadn't shaved recently. My hair looked wild, like tidal waves. I patted down it down with my hands and so followed my reflection. The two of us wore the same t-shirt and sweat-pants we had been wearing for days.

The ballot counting continued for days. The Tactile were in the lead, but the margin was narrow. Only a handful of states were left uncalled. Multiple lawsuits were filed in the Authority's name against the states. I couldn't handle hearing anymore baseless speculation and decided to cut myself off from the news until the evening. Surely if something important happened I would get a text.

I left the prison of my apartment to take a walk. Across the street was a dog park. The creatures wiggled and barked, rolled, and galloped. So many pandemic puppies. The animal shelters facilitated the adoption of a record number of dogs during the pandemic. It was an interesting coping method to fight bore-dom, isolation, and anxiety. A way to distract from the dread. I found dogs to be too dependent and eager. Unlike me, they didn't like being left alone.

I headed east to the park. The sidewalk before me was bro-ken, and the steep edges reminded me of the flat irons. I used to trip over those when I ran at night. I would fall in and out of running. It was one of those things I cycled through, obsessing over at first, then abandoning for months on end. I didn't un-derstand the draw to physical activity. I preferred the activity of the mind and thought it to be superior. When I did run, my preference was running through the park at night, along the dirt path carved into the grass. I would smoke a bit of cannabis first. When I would run, the distance gave way to darkness such that I could only see so far ahead. Glittering sidewalk lamp posts dotted the darkness receding into the stars. I would let my head explore all the hidden crevices of itself as I pushed my physical limits. In the limited sight, the silence of sound, and with the movement of my body, I felt completely occupied. When I'd return to my apartment, the feeling would fade, and the dread would shine in. What was so simple in the moonlight by the morning never is.

The park itself had an interesting past, and bodies were likely still submerged there. There could be piles. I was comforted by their presence. I felt protected. I also liked the idiosyncrasy of a scene where lively people danced and played over the hidden graves on warm summer days. But it was colder now, so I was mostly alone in my walk. The orange dust frosted the grass unfettered by the disturbance of people.

I took the dirt path that encircled the park. As I walked, I noticed the potato-shaped lumps spotting the otherwise uniform ground. I moved closer to see. They were the bodies of squirrels that had been infected. I recoiled and returned to the path. I scanned the landscape and realized the larger mounds were rabbits. The park was no longer so pleasant. I exited the next chance I could and felt the gentle whisper of the orange plague blowing gently on my neck.

I made my way back, unsure of how I would fill the rest of my time. Time became such a burden. I tried to use it wisely by expanding my skill set. I held strong the American axiom of productivity. I watched lectures on economics and engineering, read books on leadership, and tried to hone my cooking skills. None of it felt meaningful or worthwhile.

At my apartment, I turned on the television intending to get the latest margins. Yet, the television seemed to no longer be connected to the internet. I checked my phone and saw that I had no internet or reception. Curious, I inspected the modem but had no clue how to fix it. I tried restarting, unplugging, and waiting. No luck. Perhaps a break from the news would benefit me. I resigned to reading.

The internet and reception did not return. I had no means of connecting to the outside world. I thought about walking over to a friend's place to see if I could call the cable company to fix the issue. Yet I didn't know their apartment numbers and relied on my phone to call upon arrival. I thought of Sophie. She would have been my first stop. In death, she became frozen in my view, unable any longer to fend off my interpretation. In life, she would be able to do something to manage this impression, but now she existed only as I preserved her. I hoped I did her justice.

I went to her apartment anyway, to ask whoever lived there now if they had been experiencing similar issues. No one answered. I tried my other neighbor with the same result. Yet I could hear movement in the room. I returned to my apartment, retreating to the balcony to read. Outside, the weather was calm. Typically, the air was filled with an orchestra of dogs barking, but today this was replaced with stillness.

Before long the silence was broken with the melody of a distant siren. I could hear a muffled voice shouting through a megaphone. It took a few moments for me to distinguish the words. It seemed to be getting louder.

"FEDERAL MANDATE. COMPLETE QUARANTINE SHUT DOWN EFFECTIVE IMMEDIATELY. STAY IN YOUR HOMES AND WAIT FOR FURTHER INFORMATION."

The voice repeated this phrase continuously as the police SUV meandered through the streets. The vehicle's light bar glowed red, blue, and white. Within a few minutes, it passed, and stillness resumed. I wondered at the legitimacy of the appeal. It seemed an odd way to communicate such a dire message. Perhaps the internet and cell service were down for more than just me. It was the weekend, so it didn't matter much. But come Monday, I'd need the outage to lift. There were meetings scheduled.

I could see no one on the streets from my balcony. No one on balconies across the way. No sign of life. I imagined for a moment I was alone in the world. That everyone else had simply vanished. Since I had been so secluded already it didn't seem so different or unfamiliar. I felt I could breathe a little deeper. I spotted a man leaving his apartment across the street. I hesitated a moment, then resolved to call out.

"Hey! You know what is happening? Is your internet and reception out too?" I yelled toward the man. The stranger paused to listen.

"Yeah, it seems out in our building," he replied nonchalantly. His voice was raised to cross the distance.

"Did you hear the police? To stay inside indefinitely?" I prodded for more information. It was my only chance.

"Odd. No, I did not."

I briefly explained what I had seen for the stranger's awareness. The man had crossed the street to better hear me. The stranger agreed that what happened was unusual but ultimately continued on his way. Perhaps he was one of the many who predicted the pandemic would soon die out. They felt no obligation to make any changes in their habits yet.

Chapter 14

Personal lines of communication were not reestablished. Select essential businesses could stay open, but most had shut down. Travel ceased completely in order to contain the spread, but also to clear space for mass Emissary Orange removal. Sweepers were considered essential work, but there weren't enough of them to battle the mass. What was removed would return.

The first week after the outage was fettered with violence and riots. The residents were scared, confused, and alone. They turned to the streets, breaking windows, spray painting, and fire starting. Broken glass glittered on the sidewalks under the Colorado sun. Windows were covered with plywood to prevent further damage. I had even seen a few cars flipped over and aflame. Overall, there was a sense of lawlessness. Yet as quickly as it erupted, it subsided. It was as if they had released all the rage of the year in those few days. People then settled back into seclusion. Everyone eventually fell in line because there was really no way of doing otherwise.

I hadn't worked since the communication outage. I had no idea if the outage was connected to the shutdown. I speculated it could be a terrorist attack or a tactic to keep people inside.

I wondered how my family was doing back in Chicago. I hoped they were well and safe. I thought of my friends in Denver. So close yet so far. I thought of Evie.

I had gotten desperate in the last few weeks. With nothing to do, nowhere to go, and no one to talk to. I felt like a caged animal. I passed my time at my windows watching the droves of newly homeless wander the streets. The police would attempt to corral and move them, citing them for violating the quarantine. Yet they had nowhere to hide. Nowhere to stay safe. Occasionally the Sweepers would come to clear off the recent growths. I watched them with hoses and wide brooms, pushing and scrubbing.

The worst part was not knowing how the election turned out. Did the outage prevent the count? Was an Authority decided? Who was it? The months of build-up was held in suspense locked and caged. The mobile announcement at the start of this said the shut was a Federal mandate. Did that mean the president ordered this? Nonetheless, these fears had begun to be replaced with more urgent and present concerns.

The increased police presence had led to the widespread arrest of quarantine violators. Before the lockdown, the prisons already had record numbers of cases of Emissary Orange. After the lockdown, I imagined how much worse it could have gotten. The prisons couldn't likely even hold all they arrested. I would notice violators who had previously been arrested back on the same street days later. Eventually, though, I wouldn't see any of them again. For the sentence of imprisonment was tantamount to a death sentence, due to the high viral transmissions in the prisons. It affected the guards as it did the prisoners. For once impartial justice reigned in the penitentiary.

One day I had a visitor. I was reading in the living room, and I heard a thwacking noise and saw the edge of movement through the glass door to the patio. I got up and approached the door. Thwack. It was a glob of Emissary Orange hitting the building.

"Hey!" I yelled crossly. I poked my head out the door.

"Cayden!" The man yelled. I went out to the patio and leaned over the railing to look down. It was Simon.

"What are you doing! Don't throw that! Or touch it for that matter," I cautioned.

"Can I come up?"

I didn't want to let him in. He clearly was not taking the growth seriously, but at the same time, this man was my friend.

"Dude," Simon declared.

"Simon. I'm sorry I can't let you up. You should get home immediately. It's not safe."

"Then let me in!"

"What's going on? Do you need help?" I scanned my surroundings.

"You must come over! We are going to emulsify Orange tonight. You have to try it. Greatest high ever." He was shifting erratically in place and his volume was just a touch too loud. He kept looking around him, his head bouncing left and right as he spoke. He oozed aggression.

"Simon. You need help. That shit is not safe."

"So, you're a no then for tonight. Typical."

"Simon, this isn't you. What are you doing? You care about your family and friends. You aren't this high-chasing addict." It seemed he had adopted the other's objectifying label as a substitute for his unselfconscious self. His reputation was no longer serving him well.

"As long as we are willing to do anything to remain alive, we might as well be in shackles." Simon countered.

"This is for the health and safety of you and the ones around you. This is not that large of a burden. I agree with your sentiment but not your point."

"Got it. 'No.'" Simon turned and left.

I only left my house to get groceries and alcohol. Such activities were no longer just chores but had evolved into adventures. On one such adventure, I had left my apartment and the halls were empty. No one in the lobby. The windows in the lobby reached to the ceiling, framing the meandering parade of people. I popped my head out of the door to get a better view. A police vehicle was shepherding the people forward. I backed inside, having decided it was better to wait for it to pass than to try to cut through it.

A woman with her child milled along the street, almost unaware of their surroundings. Among the sleepwalkers, someone screamed, "Where are we expected to go?" An old man pushed a shopping cart down the street. There was a small group of protestors amid the wandering herd. They wore matching t-shirts with hand-painted letters stating, "WE ARE NOT FREE." They looked weary and passed silently, solemnly. The cop car rolled by sirens sounding.

I exited after the car had passed. I made my way quickly to the bridge, keeping my mask up and my head down. I knew I could be stopped at any time by the police for being outside my home. I didn't want to deal with justifying my journey. As I approached the bridge, I noticed a figure stationed by the stairs. By size, it seemed male, and the form almost vibrated in place. I wondered if the nausea was returning. As I drew near, I could see the man's features more clearly. He was laughing hysterically in place. I put my head down and walked carefully around him. I seemed to have gone unnoticed.

I crossed the bridge over the empty highway. It was unusually quiet until I heard an amplified voice. I could see a crowd formed where the road dead-ended at the train tracks. It was packed near the front, but socially distanced near the back and sides. The density correlated inversely with mask-wearing. The man at the front had their full attention and the crowd stood still. He wore a bright orange robe which demanded attention.

I listened in from an obscured spot on the bridge. The man was spouting a religious sermon. He claimed that the disease was God's reckoning with man and that we must repent. He beckoned for man to condemn their false idols and to unite in repentance to the Lord. I wondered if he meant their political abstractions when a trash can erupted in flame. I took that as my cue to keep moving and weaved through the congregation. With no people driving except the police, people littered the streets. I paused just outside the store.

I reached into my pocket and removed a few bills. I had some money saved up, but I was still unemployed. Or at least I thought I was since I had no way to contact the company. I had thought about driving out there to see if anyone had come in or to see if I could find my manager. But the constant stream of police vehicles shouting orders deterred this notion.

After picking up a few necessities, I returned to find that the crowd by the bridge had expanded substantially. The preacher's crowd began filling up city blocks. Perhaps it was his charm or rhetoric. Or maybe people just had nothing else to do or nowhere else to go. The crowd was still divided by precautionary level, but they were all united in attention. I scanned the crowd and noticed a familiar face. It was Evie. She was dressed in blue scrubs and stood in the back with the socially distanced group. I made my way over and greeted my friend.

"Evie! Hey, how are you? Are you doing okay?" I questioned. She smiled with her eyes when our gazes met.

"Oh Cayden! It is so good to see you. I'm surviving. Are you well?" Evie replied. She sounded tired but genuine. Her scrubs lent me to believe she was either coming from or going to work.

"What's going on here? The police are everywhere. I'm sure some will be passing soon enough," I cautioned. Evie took my arm and started leading me through the crowd.

"Let's get away from the crowd," she said, turning back to meet my glance. We took the bridge over the tracks toward my place. Evie paused to look back at the crowd. She could see a few trashcan fires and police cars in the distance. It reminded her of the poverty of her childhood. She shuddered and pulled me forward. But we both stopped short.

We had almost walked into a demonstration. People marched through the street chanting, "FOUR MORE YEARS." I wondered if they had gotten some news I hadn't. More likely they were just fanatics. Even if the news were still on, it seemed that the immediate needs of survival would out shadow political presence. We continued again in silence, and it remained that way until we entered the apartment. I closed the door behind us.

"Evie." We hugged.

"What were you doing over there? You could have been arrested. What's going on?" I continued.

"It's true. What he's saying. We must repent," she almost whispered.

"Do you think the growth is the fault of humanity?" I asked.

"I do. I believe that we are to blame for all of our sins. For destroying this beautiful world and for fighting with one another."

"Evie…" I sighed.

"I know what you're going to—"

"Let me finish. Evie, I know we do not believe some of the same things. But I want you to know that I understand that you are hurting now, and I want to help you."

"Thanks," Evie sighed.

"You should listen to him. He makes very good arguments. Many people who didn't believe changed their minds," she sustained.

"Perhaps, but I think you are confusing imminence with transcendence…or functions with actions…How have you been otherwise? Have you been able to contact anyone? Have you been safe? Have you heard anything about the election?" I responded.

"I've been enduring. I work all the time but at least it keeps my mind busy. I don't have communication access, but I do hear a lot from the patients," Evie began. She paused, looking around the room. My apartment was minimalist and tidy. It was handsome but cold.

"Turns out walkie-talkies work just fine, but those are distance limited and sold out everywhere. I have heard many stories of people trying to escape too."

"Escape?" I looked inquisitively at her. My eyebrows scrunched, my head tilted slightly, and my mouth pulled to one side.

"Yes. Escape from this. The neighborhoods have been blocked off with concrete traffic barriers, so cars are out of the question. There are a few select routes for resupply, but those are heavily guarded. Escape that way results in gunshot wounds."

"Has anyone come in with information about the outside? How far does this go? I don't know if there is anywhere to escape to." I continued.

"Some of them were just trying to get home. Others went to find refuge with family or friends after becoming displaced. Some really needed to know what happened to the election."

"I see."

"Anyway. I need to get back. How do we stay in contact?" Evie began shuffling through her purse.

"Meet me Thursday. 3 AM. On the stairs in Commons Park."

"What day is today?"

"Good Question. Let's meet after three nights pass."

"Done," stated Evie.

I leaned in and kissed Evie's cheek. She closed her eyes and her head dropped ever so slightly. It caught her breath. She smiled and her eyes met mine.

"Three nights pass," she said. "Three nights pass."

Chapter 15

I snuck out cloaked in the darkness of night. I wore dark clothing, walked fast, and kept my head down. The stairs were sheltered by architectural design features and high sidewalls. They were spiraled stairs to nowhere in the middle of the park. I approached the structure but was still alone. I walked up to the top where the stairs peaked and continued back down on the other side. I used my vantage point to search the rest of the park for visitors. Evie was nowhere to be found. I was alone, but for a few police officers ambling around the park entrance and the tents.

I waited in the cool, crisp night for an hour. It was the conversion between day and night, and it made me feel anxious. I played out worst-case scenarios in my mind. Snow had begun to fall from the sky, stinging as it touched my bare skin. At four, I returned home disillusioned but maintained my resolve to find Evie. I would wait until 5 PM to catch the afternoon flux of people, hiding in the crowds and pretending to be returning from work. I had found a grocery apron for the local grocer on the street that I would bring it with me to aid my story. In the meantime, I waited. At the window, I read the homemade signs on newspaper and printer paper that littered the windows of the buildings around me.

"We are in this together!" "REELECT"

"LeT uS OuT!"

"Why is everyone yelling?"

I reflected on my time in quarantine. The plague forced inactivity of the body, but not of the mind. I reveled in the solace of my memories while in exile. I had begun to feel as if I was drifting through life. It all felt so meaningless. And in that meaninglessness, looking for meaning, I found the absurd. Was light a wave or a particle? I tried to speed up the march of time, but realizing this was futile, I resolved to be content to live for the day. I was left to savor the bitter sense of freedom stemming from total deprivation.

While I had to ration my resources, I was wealthy in terms of disconnected entertainment. Not that I wanted to partake in those doings. But I had a bookshelf full of books I always intended to read. I had four 1000-piece puzzles, a keyboard, and art supplies. I also had an old mp3 player that brought me back to 1994. I even owned a sewing machine. Yet all of this was not enough to maintain sanity as a prisoner. All those activities felt absurd and irrelevant.

My remembering was interrupted by a noise at the front door. I stepped away from the window and approached the door. I walked cautiously of my footsteps and the associated noise. Peeping through the observation hole, I saw only the empty hall. But again, the sound. I placed my hand on the doorknob and opened it slowly. As I cracked the door open, a tiny head popped into the apartment just above the floor. It was Sophie's cat.

I had bought food for the cat months ago when I had last encountered the feline. It sat in my closet waiting for our next encounter. The cat was orange, in fur and in the light dusting of Emissary Orange that covered it. It meowed and looked up at me, imploring me to open the door. It looked desperate, matted, and thin.

I cracked the door, and the cat ran inside and curled up on top of a sweater I had left on the ground. I grabbed some gloves, donned my mask, and picked up the cat, heading to the bathroom. The cat wore a dainty pink collar with a tag saying "I'm Lauren. Please return to Sophie" and listed a phone number. I filled up the bathtub and cleansed the cat.

Afterward, I threw out the contaminated towel, poured food and water for the cat, then bleached the bathroom. I took my own shower, and resumed my spot at the window, now with the company. As I took my seat, I could see a handful of people on the street wandering. Within moments, a scream interrupted the still afternoon.

"Help! Help me! Please," a woman screamed. I rushed to my balcony, leaning over the railing to try to figure out from where the sound was coming. I had no clue. I looked down at the people on the street. They had paused at the disruption looking at one another.

"Help me please!"

I still couldn't distinguish where it was coming from. The people below continued back on their ways. I ran down to the street to see if I could hear better and find the woman. But on my arrival, I heard no more. Had the people become accustomed to cries for help? Or did they refrain from aiding due to the quarantine? I wasn't sure what to do or how I could help.

Eventually, I returned for my apron and set out to find Evie. She didn't live very far, but every step outside was a risk of arrest and/or infection. When I arrived at Evie's place, I had to wait for someone to get me past the front door. I hoped Evie was home and safe, but I felt a pit in my stomach, causing me to slightly hunch. The problem was I couldn't just wait there.

No reason allowed people to be out and waiting. So, I took laps around the block, and within six laps I found a way in.

Evie lived in an apartment that was built in the seventies and updated in the nineties. The pool had been filled and used as a parking lot. Balconies hung over the parking lot, facing the cars. At her door, I noted the room number, so I could buzz in the future. I knocked with anticipation but only silence greeted me. I knocked again. Nothing. I tried the doorknob, but the door was locked. I scanned the door and floor for any clues. At last, I tried lifting the ceiling tiles above the door. After the third tile I tried, a key fell to the floor. I opened the door to Evie's apartment, calling out her name as I entered. Her place was tidy, and immediately I noticed a note on the kitchen table:

"Cayden,

If you find this, I apologize for missing our meeting. Something urgent came up that I need to tend to. I am pregnant, and I need to get medical attention. I am not prepared to have a child, and I do not want to raise one in the world we inhabit presently. I am making my way to Boulder. John found me a way out!

Love always,

Evie"

Boulder was about 27 miles northwest of Denver, nestled in the front range of the Rocky Mountains. It would have been accessible by vehicle, but for the barricades and surveillance. I wondered how long-ago Evie left for her journey. Perhaps I could catch up. She shouldn't be making this journey alone, even in normal circumstances. I wondered which route she was taking when I noticed her bike was missing.

I ran home, packed a backpack, and went to track down John to see if he had any information. There used to be an abortion clinic in downtown Denver, but with the lack of federal protection and the shutdown, abortion clinics were folding at a record rate. A few hundred miles journey to get to a clinic was not unusual, according to Evie's hospital connections. Beyond that, endless laws were regulating what information must be provided, timing, facility maintenance, waiting periods, and parental involvement. This should be a simple procedure between a physician and the patient, but society claimed ownership of women's bodies. Like the world itself, representation of the world is the work of men; they define it from their point of view, which they mistake as absolute truth.

I thought of the vice-authoritarian opponent. The authoritarian opponent was not noteworthy, but his running mate was. She was a black and Indian woman, the first to run for her role. Her womanhood was an advantage to some, a disadvantage to others. Either way, she still served as the other to her male running mate. There was hope her position would rectify the gaping disparities in women's rights. If she won, that is.

I took my bike and took the trail following the creek. John lived in Washington Park. Halfway, I ran into a checkpoint. There were two officers and a traffic barrier. I slowed and dismounted my bike, pulling my backpack in front of me. The men asked me for my reason for being outside of my home. I told them I was headed to work, a grocery store in Wash Park. The men hesitated, looking at one another. I asked if I could go into my backpack to show them my apron. Approval was always needed for motion when it came to cops. They agreed, and I showed them the dirty apron. I noticed it had a light orange footprint on it. The men let me go.

As I continued, I could feel the cool air push over the creek. The retaining walls on each side of me boasted new graffiti. Most were memorials of those who had been lost. Angels crosses, and prayers filled the expanse, while rough rushed letters vandalized over top. "TOO MANY," it said in bold orange paint. The shrubs below were bare and sharp, almost oblique. Some fast-food containers littered the ground, and I dodged them and the diving pigeons as I rode. I could see the tops of buildings peering above the retaining walls.

I took the ramp toward John's and arrived at his apartment a few minutes later. I walked up the metal staircase exposed to the environment. Snow had begun to fall. I knocked on the door and waited. A moment later John burst out of his apartment and cheerfully greeted me.

"Cayden! What are you doing here? How are you?" John seemed well.

"Did you talk to Evie? Where did she go?" my words were rushed.

"Yeah, come in." John turned, looking into his apartment, then opened the door.

"Cayden," It was Evie's voice.

I rushed inside to confirm. It was her.

Evie showed up at John's apartment a few days prior. She had tried to find Cayden, but she didn't remember what floor he lived on. Evie had only been there a handful of times. She even went to his apartment and managed to get through the lobby. But she wandered the floors in hope of something familiar, but instead, they were only familiar to each other. It was almost dizzying. When she couldn't get to me, she had gone to John. John had spent the last few months working as a Sweeper. He had previously been a schoolteacher, but since the orange this no longer became possible. At first, schools moved to remote learning, but the communication outage forced closure. So, he turned to the only option he found—sweeping. He had made his own protective gear out of plastic and trash bags, tape, and fabric. Every day he took to the streets to scrape and spray the orange enemy. In doing this he had made the rounds. His job took him to all parts of the city, and he frequented some of the posts, barracks, and gates. There he had made a few acquaintances and learned of the existence of an "organization" handing lucrative business.

When Evie arrived at John's, he was not home. She waited an hour for his return, sitting and leaning against his door. She spent her time thinking of the growth inside of her. She didn't know how long she had been pregnant, but she hoped it was still early enough to legally obtain the necessary procedure. Evie could not have a child now, she needed to help the innumerable populace affected by the disease. She also did not know who the father was. She had been attacked as society's abstractions of compassion and faith had turned to pure pleasure-seeking hedonism.

Evie had been walking home from work in the late evening and had passed a man leaning against a building. He followed her as she moved past him, and at the next opportunity pulled a gun to her back grabbing her mouth to cover her screams. He pulled her into the alley and pushed her into a clearing amongst the orange mold. He violated her and left her there crying. She felt fear for her life replace the persistent anxiety of recent existence. The anxiety of freedom-based choice had been taken from her.

She would survive this, though, as she survived it all. This though, left her a shell of herself, unable to fill the void inside that man created the moment he filled her. The worst thought of it all was that this child could be his. She felt something evil growing inside of her, something born of hate and rage. It felt alien, and as it was eating her alive.

When John arrived, it was clear Evie had been crying. He welcomed her inside and she told him of her plight. John made her lunch and listened to her story. Evie stared at the knife John was using to cut tomatoes, and it caused her to pause. She felt anxiety overcome her. She longed momentarily to run that blade across her wrists. Evie felt anxious not because she was in danger of hurting herself, but because she felt she had the freedom to do so. But despite that feeling, she resumed her story. John had been a compassionate listener, and he realized he may be able to help Evie.

John's connections with the contraband smugglers through his sweeping role had described similar efforts but for those in need of escape. He told Evie of this and figured he needed a few days to track down the right people. John recommended Evie stay with him until they get more information. The leave would likely be abrupt. Evie agreed and stayed.

With my arrival, Evie explained it all again. She relived the pain. John had been able to contact the "organization" and had arranged for someone to meet her later that day. She had paid a handsome sum for the effort. However, it was discounted due to John's relations. I vowed to join her on her journey. I understood her resolve and that in choosing she made it the right choice.

Within a few moments, we heard a knock at the door. We looked at one another, then John stood up to answer it. He didn't recognize the man through the peep hole, but he figured he wouldn't. John did not know who would be sent to help Evie on her journey. He only hoped they were reliable and trustworthy. John saw a man with a shaved head, pale and fidgeting. He wore a black hooded zip-up sweatshirt, and a black mask covering his mouth and nose.

John opened the door. "Alex. You must be John," said the man. John moved aside so Alex could enter. He took off his shoes and took a seat.

"Who is this?" Alex asked looking at me.

"We've got one more," said John.

"That'll be extra. One is hard enough, two is worse. And I can't make any guarantees."

"That's fine. How much?" I stated reaching for my wallet. Alex's voice sounded familiar.

"Five hundred total. It goes to pay bail for the wrongly imprisoned."

"I have only 423," I showed him the cash.

"I can help," John headed out of the room and returned shortly with the rest of the cash.

"Very well. We leave now. You have a bike, I assume?"

I nodded.

"We will bike through the neighborhoods and take no major streets. It will take about 5 hours. We meet at a medical laundromat and will get a ride from there. I've packed food and water in case we must delay the journey. Put these on." Alex handed Evie a standard-issue sweeper face shield. The band was red with the word "SWEEPER" across the forehead in white. It reminded him of a welding mask. Alex only had one. John recognized this and gave Cayden his sweeper shield from the closet.

"I can get another one. Go!" said John. He tossed the mask to me.

"Let's go. This should be sufficient disguise to be out."

The three of us biked from John's place weaving through barricades going what seemed to be haphazardly from one street to the next. We staggered through the city blocks, going through the sleepiest sections. We headed over to the highlands, past the sports arena that had been repurposed as a makeshift hospital. We saw a small crowd outside the entrance holding gift bags and signs. People in hope of seeing their loved ones despite the restrictions.

Past the arena, we took streets through the neighborhood. All was clear until we turned. We had run into an unexpected checkpoint based on Alex's facial reaction.

"Stay calm."

We dismounted our bikes, and slowly approached the barricade and service van. There were two officials there but did not appear to be police. I couldn't tell if it was the national guard or another rouge militant group. Either way, I was concerned.

"Good afternoon officers. We are headed to the site of Eta 436," Alex offered once in hearing distance.

The men looked them up and down. They didn't have on any additional protection besides the face shield. Looking down I realized we didn't even have gloves on. Surely Sweepers would be wearing gloves.

"Eta 436, eh?" said one of the officers.

"Yes, sir. Eta 436. Big pile up of Emissary Orange near the northwestern barracks."

"Eta 436, you say. Isn't that in the southwest sweeping quadrant? You folks are headed the wrong way."

Alex stood still and silent. I began to sweat, and Evie looked down at the ground.

"What do you know about quadrants, Henry?" laughed the fellow officer. "Go on ahead. Watch out for runners."

Runners. Evie and I had become runners. We smiled lightly and continued forward. After sufficient distance, the group sighed audibly. We continued to walk our bikes down the street until Alex pulled aside. He observed his surroundings and then lowered his face mask to better breathe. I immediately noticed his cleft lip and realized where I had recognized this man's voice from. This was the man who had attacked Pete, the dispensary salesman, for wearing and requiring a mask. This was who was saving them?

It was clear that Alex did not recognize me, and I wondered what I would do with this new information. Should this man be trusted? He was wearing a mask now, so perhaps he had come to his senses. I used the pause as an opportunity to learn more.

"So, what brought you into this business?" I tried to ask casually.

"Not now," Alex said shortly. "Let's keep going."

We biked through the highlands without further interruption. We passed the overpriced small homes and the empty boutique restaurants. A few Sweepers were cleaning off the sidewalk. Alex waved at them, and they waved in response. We biked for about an hour, maintaining our snaked routed through the suburbs. We eventually pulled into a strip mall, occupied with a landscaping business, an adult bookstore, a crematorium, and a laundromat. A small crowd dressed in black stood outside the crematorium. We biked around the back in the alley, stopping near an open garage door. Inside were bins filled with white fabric splotched with orange. They were medical gowns. We pushed the bikes into the garage and leaned them up against the back wall. We waited next to the white moving van.

"Wait here," said Alex. Alex left through a door near the back wall. A moment later he stepped out with company. The woman was stern-looking with short blonde hair. She wore a one-piece blue uniform with the name "Alliance Cleaning" across the front.

"This is Avery. She is going to be taking you to Boulder. You will sit in the cleaned clothes and exit once you're in the medical building utility room. She will take you from here. I will be back here tomorrow same time to collect you. Do not be late." "Welcome," Avery said, smiling through her mask. "Time to get going get in here." She pointed to the moving van. Inside were bins full of folded white fabric. Evie and I walked up the moving ramp and nestled into the bins. Avery put a few more layers of clothing on top of us.

"Here we go," we heard.

The back door of the van slammed shut and I winced. The engine started. The ride was slow and felt as if it took an eternity. Every step on the brake instilled anxiety. At some point, the vehicle stopped, and the sound of a garage door closing echoed. The van door opened, and Avery whispered, "We're here."

The two of us climbed out of the bins and threw the fallen gowns back into them. We walked down the ramp and thanked Avery for her help. She gave us instructions for us to return.

Chapter 16

We escaped from the hospital and headed toward the abortion clinic, thanking Avery for her help. The clinic was nestled up to the mountains on the western-most part of the town. We walked down the neighborhood streets. The sky was smokey and lit up orange. It was hard to tell if it was the Emissary Orange dust or a nearby wildfire. The houses were wide apart with sizeable front lawns. The houses themselves boasted modest wealth, but they cost more than they looked. You could tell by the cars. Further down we could see a sign, "Pregnancy Help Center".

"That must be it," I said pointing at the sign. Evie nodded and we approached the building, entering through the lobby. The walls were painted a light blue, and there were three empty folding chairs across from the reception desk. A young woman sat behind the desk reading. Above the desk was a cross.

"Hello. I need an abortion." Evie stated.

"Well hello there lost one. We can help you understand all your options. Please take a seat. Here is some paperwork to fill out and a brochure." Evie grabbed the documents and headed to her seat.

She began filling out the paperwork as I grabbed the brochure. I opened it up and began reading. It began with a few words of a sermon about a woman who had lost her way. She had experienced a discharge of blood that lasted twelve years. She had sought doctors and medical assistance to no avail, for she suffered greatly. The woman had heard reports about Jesus and felt that even just touching his garments would be enough to cure her. So, she did, without his permission, and Jesus searched the crowd for the offender feeling some of his power drained from his being. The woman approached Jesus, trembling with fear, and fell before him in penance. Jesus turned to her and said, "Daughter, your faith has made you well; go in peace and be healed of your disease." I flipped forward, finding the section on options available.

"Options available to you at this time:

- Adoption
- Becoming a parent
- Finding the Lord"

"Shit," I muttered. "Evie, I think—"

"Evie. We're ready for you," said the nurse as she popped through the door.

"Evie, I don't think this is—"

"Cayden don't doubt me," Evie turned and followed the nurse.

When Evie entered the room, she couldn't help but notice more religious artifacts. A poster of Jesus on the wall looked down at her, and there was a cross above the door. She changed into the gown and sat on the cold table.

The nurse entered. She introduced herself and informed Evie they would be starting with an ultrasound. She asked Evie to lay back and lifted her gown above her stomach. She massaged on a cool clear gel and used the wand to roam over her bare stomach. The nurse summoned Evie's attention to the screen next to her.

"Look at this heartbeat. This is a life. Do you understand that?" the nurse said.

"Look. I'm here for an a—"

"Yes, to find out your options. Why don't you watch one of our informational videos? If you do you get credit to the clinic store. You can buy diapers, clothing, formula—"

"Is this a certified clinic? I am here for a procedure."

"Let's get Father in here. I think he will—"

"No. This is one of those fake clinics, isn't it? Get out I'm changing and leaving," Evie pushed the woman away from her stomach.

Evie burst out of the office into the lobby where I sat anxiously. "I know," said Evie looking at me. "Wrong one."

I stood up and embraced Evie. We exited and headed north. The houses gave way to a few small businesses and those gave way as well to a graveyard. The graveyard was filled with people in black. Small groups formed circles around the holes in the ground and makeshift headstones, while those without the luxury of either congregated near the edges of the park. Funerals had evolved from elaborate religious ceremonies to something more transactional. The overabundance of bodies and the proximity to the plague caused the process to be defined by maximizing speed and minimizing risk.

Once a personal mourning event, funerals now were orchestrated assembly lines. Coffins were removed from vans in numbers. The bodies were removed from the coffins and lowered into a giant pit. As soon as the body was removed, the coffin was sanitized right there on the street and reloaded to return to the camps or morgue. Before long coffins and burials were abandoned completely.

"So much death," Evie remarked, looking at the cemetery.

"We have all been impregnated with death. It was just a matter of when it would be born," I replied.

"Oh Cayden," she said. Evie smiled behind her mask.

"It should be right up here."

When we approached the clinic, we could see demonstrators in the parking lot out front. Not many but enough. I saw about fifteen people, some handing out fliers, others holding signs. One of the signs showed a cartoon depiction of a grown fetus being ripped by the leg out of the womb. As we approached, Evie was steadfast. She marched forward on the sidewalk, then turned toward the clinic and paused.

A woman came up to her. "Do not kill your child. Murderer!" she said yelling in Evie's face. As Evie pushed, forward a man jumped in front of her "The Lord is watching!" She moved around him with the door in sight. This time they were at the right place. While Evie had her procedure, I waited in the lobby with the receptionist.

"What has been going on here in Boulder? Do you have communication?" I asked. I figured I should get an idea of the conditions here.

"From out of town? No, we don't have communications, except for the fliers."

"Fliers?" I asked.

The woman pulled a blue flier from a pile of papers on her desk. She handed it to me.

"The latest news."

The flier detailed the latest updates on the wildfires. Towns that were affected and in danger were listed. There were updates on the number of local Emissary Orange deaths. It also reaffirmed the lockdown and full quarantine with the mention of a vaccine in the works.

"What is the deal with the vaccine?" I asked.

"It's been in the works since the start. Any day now apparently." Her tone suggested otherwise.

"Do you know why there is a communication outage? Or how long it will last?" I inquired.

"No word on that." She seemed uninterested in talking, but I pushed further.

"The election?"

"Does it matter right now? We're all on our own," the women replied.

The appointment took an hour. I gave Evie a hug and the two of us left to find a hotel for the night. As we walked down the pedestrian mall, we could sense an absence. Usually, the few town blocks would host street performers that drew sizeable crowds. There had been magicians, fire dancers, balancing acts, and psychics. I wondered what they were all doing now. A few more blocks and we approached a hotel advertising vacancy.

The hotels were empty since no one could leave their homes. Then, they mainly catered to the guests who had been stuck there from out of town during the lockdown. The man at the front desk seemed surprised to see us. He gave us a room, and upon entering, Evie went directly to the bed and to sleep. I stayed up a while longer and brought a drink down to the lobby.

The lobby was empty but for a man sitting alone by the fireplace. I took a seat near him but far enough to maintain distance. The man wore a black hat and a thick wool jacket. His face boasted crevices of ancient acne scars that formed a road map on his cheeks.

"Hey there. What brings you to the hotel?" I started. "I'm Cayden."

"Martin. I'm a journalist from LA. I came into town to write an article and am now trapped here."

"I'm sorry to hear that. How have you been coping? Is there no way to get back?"

"I'm dying here. My wife is in Houston by herself. I haven't been able to contact her and have no idea if she is even still alive. The roads are blocked, and flights are down, so I have no idea how to get back. I know I must though. It is all that I can think about. The omnipotence of possibility weighs on me." The man wiped away a stray tear.

"Have you talked to the officials about your plight? Is there a legal option?" I inquired.

"I've exhausted those options and the police refuse to see me anymore."

"If you've got a bike, we are headed to Denver tomorrow. You can join us if you have cash to pay for the arrangement."

"No, no. The risk is too high."

We sat in silence, sipping our drinks. I imagined if someone I loved were kept from me by plague. Were they getting used to doing without them? Or were they wasting away emotionally as well as physically? Without communication it was impossible to verify livelihood, so the mind is left exploring the darkest crevices of possibility. Yet I was not able to comprehend this level of despair since I could not form those connections in the first place. I could not let myself depend on others for meaning.

The next day, Evie and I met Avery at the loading dock of the medical hospital. We took again our positions in the laundry bins. This time we had to wait four hours before the vehicle moved. We waited in anguish. It was hard to breathe under all the fabric. It made Evie dizzy. She was reassured only by the fact that she had finished what she had set out to do. On the road back, the van was forced to make an unscheduled stop. I held my breath. Something banged on the side of the van. We heard voices, muffled. The van door charged open, and the two of us hidden remained still. More voices. I released my breath slowly. The door slammed closed, and a moment later the car began moving.

"Shit," I released audibly.

Evie let out a muffled chuckle.

We continued down the road, and eventually, we parked and were released. Alex was not there yet but would arrive forty minutes later. He told us the risk was higher now due to newly added check points. They would need to take a longer route. I wondered if this was a ploy to get more money, but the man never got there. We made it through the suburbs without any police encounters. We paused at the ramp to the creek trail. Alex would leave them here.

"Why are you doing this?" I asked.

"Imagine there was a pill that dissolves fear of death. Would you take it?" Alex quizzed.

I stared at the man. The same man who attacked someone for wearing a mask was now helping people escape the impacts of the illness.

"Yes. I believe we shrink ourselves when we fear it. I would be able to live a more genuine life."

"No. The fear of death defines living. Without it, you cannot live."

"What does that have to do with this?"

"Everything. The plague has highlighted the commonality amongst the previously polarized masses. Such old visions of abstractions have given way, and we all face the same danger. We are all connected."

"Indeed," I replied. I also imagined that Alex made good money doing what he did, profiting from the pain. Alex tipped his head to the side and handed me a note.

"If you need my services again."

Chapter 17

My adventure with Evie had emboldened me. I wanted to venture out more but was held back by the threat of infection. I felt despondent, as most people did, but not resigned. Being back and alone, I fell into the mass appeal of acquiescence. I realized that in seclusion my senses had been heightened, and it was as if I could smell the sickly-sweet odor of the orange plague. Or perhaps that was the nausea.

I decided I would try to visit Ruth. Maybe she had a better idea of what was going on legally with this shutdown. Maybe she had some answers. Ruth lived in River North or RiNo, and the area consisted of renovated warehouse breweries and sleek apartments and condos. There were no grasses or trees to be found, and I felt the vastness of concrete formed a respectable urban dessert. In that dessert, though, was an oasis of art. For RiNo was the art district and boasted giant displays of sharp colors across the buildings, murals, and a bit of the Avant-Garde. I could take the creek path from my apartment.

When I arrived, I followed in another resident and walked to Ruth's door. I knocked twice, then heard someone moving around chains and locks. The door opened and Ruth stood there holding her baby with a pouting three-year-old wrapped around her leg. She looked disheveled and busy.

"Cayden! What are you doing here? Come in!" Ruth backed away from the door making a path for me. I removed a few toys from the couch and took a seat. Her home was snug, with thick heavy curtains softening the edges. Her furniture was fine but worn. It was as if time had eroded the sharp edges, leaving behind a sense of smooth velvet.

"Hey, Ruth. I hope I'm not bothering you. I just needed to talk to someone."

"You've been quarantining right? No contact with the orange?"

I gave her my whereabouts and interactions of the last two weeks. She did the same. She paused to evaluate, then let me in. I headed straight for the bathroom and washed my hands. "Can you talk and help me with the kids at the same time? Martin is trapped in D.C. with this shutdown, and I'm here alone with the kids. Can you entertain them while I do laundry?" With the baby still in her arms, Ruth picked up stuffed animals and placed them in a bin.

"Of course." I took the baby from Ruth and gently rocked him in my arms. I looked down at the baby with its fresh, smooth skin. The child oozed purity, and its eyes shone brightly. What I held was pure existence without essence. It felt sacred.

"Have you heard from Martin at all?" I asked. The baby cooed.

"Not a word. How would I? I miss him terribly and so do the children. I hope he is safe."

"Me too, Ruth…Have you been working at all?" I asked.

"Here and there. Luckily, I can bring the paperwork home, but it's too much to do with the kids. Most of my cases have been suffering."

"I've heard women have been dropping out of the work-force left and right due to the pandemic."

"Very much so. Here. Can you put that on the shelf?" Ruth handed me the bottle of laundry detergent.

"What cases are you working on now?"

"Mostly divorce cases. This plague has also brought down our institution of marriage. Too much time trapped together. I also have a few immigration cases and a transgender discrimination case."

"Sounds like a lot."

"Indeed. How are you doing?"

"I'm alright. I feel as if I am just surviving. But I suppose that is the best we can do these days."

"Some seem to be thriving. Have you seen Simon lately?" Ruth continued to fold laundry. The older child played with toys in the corner.

"I have. It seems he's strung out on orange."

"Fear must seem to him more bearable under these conditions than it was when he had to bear its burden alone."

"It's true, we are all in this together."

Bang. Bang. Ruth and I turned to each other. The knock was not at their door, but perhaps a neighbor's.

Bang. Bang. "Open up. Emissary Orange Agent."

"Do you know what that is?" I whispered.

"I've heard of this. They come to collect those who violate quarantine."

Ruth and I moved to the door. Ruth cracked it open, leaving the chain lock in place. The two of us peered through the crack. We could see two men in military garb and a man dressed in a white laboratory coat. The officers held a small battering ram.

"Open up or we are coming in."

Silence.

Bam! The officer swung the ram at the door, busting the doorknob right off. The door swung open with the push of an officer. The three men disappeared into the room. Next was a scream. The officers quickly reemerged with a man kicking and screaming. He coughed and choked, trying to yell for help. He was sweating through his white shirt, and his eyes were wild and orange. He called out for help, making eye contact with Ruth through the crack in the door.

I gently closed the door and looked at Ruth.

"Can they legally do that?" I asked.

"Unfortunately, they can."

"Have you heard anything about the election?"

"I have in fact. Keep this to yourself. The election is stuck in the courts. The opponent won, but the Authority continues to discredit the results and pursue legal action." Her conviction on the subject shook my confidence in my memories.

"Are you serious? He won the popular vote and the electoral college?"

"Indeed."

I felt a wash of relief cascade upon me. I was also stunned. The last four years had felt like a nightmare, and now I was going to wake up. I felt safe for just a moment.

"Was it close?"

"At first, but now, no. Although more people voted for the incumbent than for any other Authority before, besides the opponent of course."

"I had thought that all evil that is in the world was born of ignorance. Could that many people be ignorant?"

"I don't know if I prefer that or the alternative."

"Does the Authority have a chance at winning his legal battles? Is he justified?"

"The man will exploit any loophole in the system. I just hope we don't have too many."

The three-year-old toddled toward me but paused halfway there to cough. Ruth and I looked at each other with concern.

"I think it's just a cold. His eyes are clear." supplied Ruth. "It's getting late. I should get them to bed."

"And I should get back. Come by my place anytime."

I left and Ruth scanned her surroundings. The place was a mess and the children were in need. She desperately missed her husband and could use the help. Tommy, the eldest, burst out in tears. Large tears rolled down his face and pooled in the creases of his twisted mouth. Ruth picked him up and felt the heat from the small body radiate in her arms. She looked at his eyes, and what was once clear was now clouded.

She ran to the door, opened it, and yelled out for me. But I had already left. Ruth packed up her things and set out for the closest Orange facility. It was only a few blocks away but before even seeing the entrance, she saw a line and could hear the coughing. The coughing seemed to echo itself emerging at various places in the line. The three waited in line for hours before being seen. Once checked in, Ruth scanned the crowd and couldn't tell who was in the most need of help. They all looked like the walking dead.

Eventually, a nurse came out in a hazmat suit, gesturing toward her. By that time, Ruth was hungry and tired, and the baby had been fussy. The baby's muffled cries and screams echoed despite the layers of fabric covering the stroller. Tommy's fever had worsened, and his body violently trembled with each cough. But when Ruth went to follow the nurse, the woman halted. She shouted through her mask that Ruth could not join. The child had to be ripped from her arms.

Waiting further in agony, at long last Ruth was brought to a hallway with a makeshift curtained room, and nurses flooded in. Tubes and monitors, needles and pills flowed through the space between the curtains. She could hear her child's sustained screaming as she tried to get closer. The sound was unbearable to Ruth. The screams cut through her. She pushed to get back past the curtain, but two medical assistants stepped in and held her back.

"My baby!" she screamed. The curtain flapped open, and she saw the small child stiffened with limbs stretched at oblique angles. He let out a long moan, and his body curled into itself. Beeping and wheezing alternated in melody. The child started shaking violently. The mother pushed forward again but was held in place. The child stretched out again into a star under the sheets, then retracted back inward. His small chest lifted the sheet, smoothing out the wrinkles. His chest would not rise again.

Chapter 18

I walked my bike through the alley behind Ruth's. Orange mold amalgamated with the mounded snow to create an orange bubbly foam. It fizzed where it met the black top. Orange goo grew in the street cracks like throbbing tree roots. Dumpsters and garage doors lined the alley, and between them was graffiti, angular and bright. I could hear a cough resonate in the background. The evening felt still, and I listened to the water spraying from my wheels. It sounded like shimmering. Up ahead I could see lights glowing from a large cavity in the alley wall. A few people gathered round lit up by the glow and captivated by whatever was inside. As I drew closer, I leaned my bike against the wall and joined the men in the alley without reaction on their part. It was a large warehouse with a stage in the back. The same man who had preached by the railroad tracks stood upon the platform.

The man preached that now that they had all seen the plague with their own eyes, now that death was visible, they must nowadays be better apt to comprehend the message behind it. It was time they stopped trying to run in fear and to embrace the illness and its significance. His voice was softer than last time but boldened as he sustained. But the crowd was substantially smaller than the last time since this kind of performance had lost its novelty. The people had replaced normal religious practice with its less extravagant sister, superstition. These superstitions were whispered on the street and shouted from fliers.

I quietly backed away, grabbed my bike, and resumed my walk down the alley, keeping my head down. The orange and black of the ground mixed to create a tie-dye effect as I moved. I couldn't help but note though, and pause at, a side-eye glimpse of legs being dragged on the ground. A shoe wobbled on one of the feet as the figure skimmed the pavement. I raised my head and opened my eyes slowly. A Sweeper was dragging an orange victim down the street what seemed to be toward the dumpster. Orange sludge built up around the body as it was moved. The body wore trainers, jeans, and a sweater. It was stiffening as it dragged.

"Is this part of the job now?" I asked, curious about this person's actions. It was hard to tell who exactly he was talking to with all the personal protective equipment.

"Certainly." The voice said without pausing.

"Jesus," I uttered.

"Never!" a gravelly voice hissed.

The Sweeper and I exchanged glances curiously. Recognizing the mutual confusion, we looked down. The body was a man and it coughed one last time. It sagged a little deeper, and the Sweeper resumed pulling. The body cleared a path on the ground through the orange growth. The man's eyes were stuck wide-open gleaming orange. They had witnessed the man's last word, and he had chosen "never". To never submit to that which we must eventually all succumb. His last word was that of malice to the choice that all must embrace. I felt sad for the man, not for his death but for his inability to see it as part of his last opportunity to claim freedom as his own.

Death had become a regular part of our lives, and it refused to go silently. Bodies on the street were not unusual, but the Sweepers did their best to remove them judiciously. Dumpsters were overfilled, with limbs spilling over the sides. The faces of the dead were twisted and eyes alarmed. As I strolled down the alley, I wondered how many bodies filled the bins around me. Suddenly I felt worn. As if the desert sands had eroded, removing the sharp edges of feelings. No more rage or despondence, but instead a dull feeling of emptiness. There was no larger purpose but survival. This comforted me since I no longer had to grasp at meaning. Emotions lived at the surface and were easily expelled, instead of lingering deep inside rotting. Survival though meant isolation. And isolation fostered these thoughts of meaning, and I would get trapped in the cycle again.

I reached the creek path and mounted my bike. Tents bordered the water, but no one was out. The air felt thick and moist, chilling me to my core. The breeze felt cold on my hands, but my face was kept warm by the mask. I loved the city at night. The towers of lights would reflect on the empty streets causing the ground to almost glow. The skyscraper's lit windows would surround me as if I were flying among the stars. But then, those dark towers hovered like prison walls. The streetlights' change managed only the breeze's movement, to which nature balked. I wondered how long it would take for nature to reclaim it all. How long before vines would pop up through the sidewalk cracks? How long before the animals would take back the streets? How long before time was governed again by the sun?

At the apartment, a sign was posted on the lobby door that stood out among the wrinkled fliers and napkin notes. It was laminated with a bright orange border. It read, "Emissary Orange Testing available this week. See your local pharmacist for details." I shuddered. It was late, and I went inside. I would have to wait until tomorrow to find out more.

I woke up early to prepare for any lines I may experience at the pharmacy. It seemed that all people did these days was wait in line, and it made time feel sluggish. In line, I could overhear other curious people discussing the test.

"Do you think this can be trusted?" a lady asked.

"I don't know, honey. We are going to get more information." a man replied.

Another woman behind me, "Do you think they followed the science?"

"Is it mandatory?" a voice in front of me added.

There was excitement buzzing through the line, like electricity running through cables. I was cautiously curious. A man stepped out from the front of the line and cupped his hands around his mouth. He wore a blue apron and yelled out at the line.

"Hello everyone. If you are here about the testing, please listen up. It comes in in two days. You will need insurance. The average cost is $300. We have limited supplies."

Overlapping voices overpowered the man as he continued to speak. "How are we supposed to afford that!?", "Limited supplies!? What do you mean!?", "Is more coming?", "Can we trust it?". The employee struggled to get back the attention of the crowd.

"Hello everyone." He repeated the speech twice more. It was clear no more information was to be had, and the crowd began to disperse. Like food rations, the testing and eventually a vaccine would be first in the hands of the wealthy, then that of the poor. While the growth was impartial, the treatment was not. Poor families were suffering, while the rich went short of practically nothing. Worse yet, poverty taught resignation. I thought of Alex. Worse come to worse, Alex can help me. But most couldn't afford such luxuries.

I walked home, passing abandoned restaurants and bars. Windows were boarded-up, doors were locked, and the chairs were upside down on the tables. The bright sunlight brought outwears and flaws of the décor, which were usually hidden with dim mood lighting. I paused at a building, noticing the black charring around the boarded-up windows. It appeared to have been a fire. I stepped back and noticed a bland sign above the door, announcing "Chinese Food". Spray painted across the charred siding were the words "This is your fault". I had heard that people were acting out against Asians due to the connection with Emissary Orange, but it was different seeing it in person. It felt personal. I wondered if the fire was an act of arson. Crime tape suggested so. The yellow band popped when contrasted against the black soot.

I felt weary of the plague. Weary of the precautions, the cleaning, the bleach. I was tired of masks and gloves. I felt I should fight for my survival but if I ceased caring for anything outside that, what was the use of fighting? I continued through the neighborhood, taking a longer route home. Some of the homes were decorated with holiday lights and figures. They looked gaudy in the daylight, but I imagined it in the beauty of night. It was nearing the holiday season and I had all but forgotten. From fliers and the police rounds, they were not to celebrate with anyone outside of their households. Not that that mattered much to me since all my family was back in Chicago. Normally I would fly back for the holidays but not this year.

I had spent every Christmas of my life with my parents until this point, except once. When I took the year to travel, I celebrated Christmas and the New Year in Buenos Aires. A group from the hostel, including a quiet Frenchman, a coy Italian man, and a blonde Danish woman, had found a meetup group online for travelers and decided to join. It was in a large, mostly empty apartment with a wide Juliette balcony overlooking the city. We met a few others and went out to a nightclub. I danced all night with the beautiful Danish woman, and she let me stay the night. The following morning the group reconvened for Chinese food. This would be nothing like that.

Back at home, I sat out on my balcony trying to figure out what to do with myself. It was as if I had no future. I looked down at my hands. On the arm of the chair, I noticed a glob of Emissary Orange, remnants from Simon's visit. I studied it for a moment and reflected on what little I knew about it. I knew the growth came in two forms. The first was characterized as a light powder or dust. The second was an amorphous blob, slimy and viscous. Whether it could transition between the two forms was a mystery. I held my breath behind my mask as my gloves contacted the form. I again felt that same vibration. I took the sample, put it on a slide, and went to my microscope. It was child size and had been a thrift store white elephant gift, but it functioned fairly well.

I turned the switch and the microscope light turned on. I refocused the microscope on the almost transparent edges. I moved the slide around to try to find a pattern, but there was none. No cells repeating, no similar features. The more I zoomed the more detail I saw. It was tons of tiny fractal cells freely swimming in a pool of clear gel, which seemed to loosely hold it all together. I saw endless shades of orange. Each cell was unique and free to grow.

I wondered about the powder, and if it would look the same up close. I had no idea how to get my hands on it. If the powder version had hallucinatory effects when ingested a certain way, Simon would know about it and have tried it. Or perhaps Alex was trafficking orange as well as novelty goods and runners. Or, I concluded, maybe I could create it. In the meantime, I split the rest of my sample onto five slides and placed them in a plastic container on the counter.

Chapter 19

The next day I conducted various experiments to aid in passing the time. I heated and cooled the subject. I added and removed pressure. I measured it for volume, mass, and calculated its density. I added salt to one, alcohol to the other, and set one on fire. I left one more as a control. The subject was poked, cut, stirred, and blended using whatever was available in my kitchen. Keeping an oral journal throughout the experiment duration, I observed them at all phases under the microscope. Then bleached my entire kitchen.

In reviewing progress, I could see no difference between the subjects over time, but they all looked a little drier. I watched them for an hour as the masses slowly dried up and dissolved into grains. Under the microscope, I saw millions of tiny fractal workers colliding and sharing, organizing and aligning. In the finality of the symmetry, the small sample vibrated and separated into identical grains. It had transformed, but nothing I had done had affected this process. It was as if it were ruled by time.

Time, I thought. I had only my watch and the microwave to tell me the time. Except I realized that wasn't true. In contemplating time, I realized I had another device to exploit—my car radio. I dropped the experiment and ran down to the covered garage. I found my car, but the battery was dead for lack of use. As I turned the keys, the car sputtered and stopped. Static rose over the radio for a moment before dying off. A moment of hope. I grabbed some tools from the trunk and began the surgical process of removing the radio box.

I took the assembly up to my apartment and collected supplies—a soldering iron, a power source, and crimps. I soldered the exposed wires and clipped the device to my old power source, which I had used to play with circuits. Connecting the system to some old computer speakers, white noise began to fill the room. Success. I rolled through the stations in search of any sign of life. White noise. Static. Buzz. Then hope.

"...Emissary Orange is now the deadliest plague known to man. It has killed 2.3 million people, and 108.5 million are infected, approximately. Stay in your homes and avoid contact with the orange and those who have encountered it. Cyberattacks have shut down most forms of communication. Vaccines are in the works. Today is January 28th, 2021. Emissary orange is now the deadliest—"

I listened to the broadcast repeat itself over and over.

I changed the channel.

"The election is fraught with fraud. Thousands of ballots of dead individuals were counted for the opponent. A recount is demanded..."

Since only a few had radios available, information, I gleamed, would have to be spread by word of mouth. Those with access would spread the news, be it true or false, and it would morph as it passed from individual to individual. What started as a warning could end as praise. It was a whole new test of trusting your sources. As I listened to the nonsense pouring from the airwaves, I could feel a sense of throbbing in the air, like it had a pulse. I heard a popping noise come from the kitchen. When I went to investigate, I noticed nothing unusual, until I looked at the scale. I checked my last recorded data point for mass and compared it to the current value. I found that the sample of orange on the scale had expanded in its containers, popping open the lid. The creature had transformed back from a diminished pile of powder to a throbbing, expanding goo. I turned on the scale and checked the mass again. Sure enough, it grew by a tenth.

I turned the radio back to the first station, letting it repeat in loops, and observed the samples over time. The air seemed to settle slightly. The tense pulsing had subsided, and I watched the goo slowly begin morphing back to its prior form over time. It was by no means a quick reaction, but there was at least a correlation. Perhaps they were affected by noise. But this made no sense.

There had to be something more to this. I took various objects around my apartment and experimented with the effects of noise on the orange. Clapping, banging, yelling, nor white noise seemed to have any effect. I tried next speaking aloud. I repeated what the first broadcast had said and saw the goo softly sink into itself. Then I repeated the second broadcast on loop and watched the goo expand and throb ever so slightly. I repeated individual words from the broadcasts and studied the effect, which was none. Something about the string of sounds, the phrases themselves seemed to cause change in the mass. Just as our human minds are molded by them. I tried repeating the first and second phrases in French, to see how these sounds affected the reaction.

"L'élection est pleine de fraudes. Des milliers de bulletins de personnes décédées ont été comptés pour l'adversaire. Un recomptage est demandé."

Mass growth detected.

"L'émissaire Orange est maintenant la peste la plus meurtrière connue de l'homme. Il a tué beaucoup de personnes et encore plus sont infectées, environ. Restez chez vous et évitez tout contact avec l'orange et ceux qui l'ont rencontrée. Les cyber-attaques ont interrompu la plupart des formes de communication. Les vaccins fonctionnent. Nous sommes le 28 Janvier 2021."

. It shuddered and shrank, crystallizing on the surface.

"Nous sommes le 28 Janvier 2021."

The mass deflated slightly.

I couldn't believe my eyes. It was as if the mass understood language and reacted to it. But what distinguished expansion rates?

"Today is not January 28th, 2020." Bloat.

I experimented further, alternating between simple truths and falsehoods. I leveraged some rusty Spanish and German language skills to further test. In the end, my conclusion was unbelievable. The orange seemed to feed on falsities and diminish with fact. Could it be a plague of misinformation that was killing us off? More and better studies would be needed for substantiated conclusions.

I grappled with the unlikely correlation, but further experimentation seemed to verify the results. How did it feed on misinformation if we as humans can't even differentiate truth? Even if we could, we cannot just cancel the voices of the misinformed. We must educate. But human beings cannot be adequately explained in terms of the fundamental physical constituents of the universe. Truths do not apply to humans. Maybe it had more to do with authenticity? Truth measures the attitude or passion with which I appropriate. So perhaps it fed on belief, on those who chose to disbelieve?

And even if this were true, how would we spread this information without opening the doors to additional misinformation? If communications were up, we'd be fighting an uphill battle. With them down, we could not spread news of the solution. And how do we get this information out to everyone, and equally?

Furthermore, this means people could be passing on the infection without even realizing it.

I knew I had to test it more. How would it react to subjectivity? To sarcasm? To known unknowns? What was its truth? What sort of suppression was this? The anxiety began to set in again, and questions echoed in the hollows of the self. I had been focused on this effort too long and had lost perspective. I need to talk to someone who could help.

I resolved to see Ruth, as she had connections to officials, both respected and not. I saw her sitting at the window of her apartment from the street, but once at her door, there was only silence in response to my call. I knocked again and beckoned her response. I could hear a low grunt and the door pushed forward against the doorway. I pushed lightly from my side, feeling a momentary balance of weight. I could feel her there.

"Go away."

"It's me, Cayden. Are you okay? I've got news about the orange you need to hear."

"Okay what?" she softened ever so slightly.

"What's going on? Are you sure you are okay?"

"No, Cayden. Tommy is gone. Emissary Orange."

I couldn't believe it. I had seen the small child recently, and just like that, another data point for the statistics.

"I'm so sorry," was all I could say.

"Tell me. What is the news?" she offered after the silence.

I told her what I knew, and she remained silent until the end. I could still feel the weight of her body against the door. I wished I could hug her. This was the first death of someone I had known and loved personally. I knew my bubble was not immune, but it still shocked me.

"But what about Tommy? He can barely talk, let alone lie! It doesn't fit."

"Children escape the anguish of freedom and the sense of complete and profound responsibility it brings with it. They are not yet capable of leaving their mark on the world."

"Do you mean to say that authenticity cannot be achieved by the innocent?"

"Perhaps. Do you know anyone who can help communicate the word? I'm not confident in the results but it's something."

"Yes, I know who to bring this to. If it holds any weight, I will let you know. Leave your data. Stay safe, Cayden."

Next, I went to the police. I ran out onto the street, cold without a jacket. I headed to the park, moving straight toward the police posted there.

"Sir, I believe I have found out dire information regarding the growth of Emissary Orange. This needs to get out."

"Is that so?" the man asked, looking skeptical.

"Yes, sir. I've found that it reacts to sound. To phrases more specifically. It seems to feed on misinformation."

"Huh."

"I can prove it. Please just get me to someone who can help."

"And who are you exactly?"

"Cayden Freeman. I'm an engineer and scientist. I have data you will want to see."

"I'm Officer Dean Stadum. Alright, let's head down to the station and go from there."

We walked in silence until we reached the station, 8 blocks down. It felt odd being outside and not worrying if the police were going to find me. I was justified for being out and it felt like freedom. The pace was slower than I could bear, but I contained the energy bursting inside of me like a pressure vessel. When we arrived, the station felt full but sleepy. Like the weight of the disease had increased the air's viscosity.

"All, gather here. We've got a new theory for the illness."

I explained to them what I had found, and I showed them my data and one of the samples. I put the sample down on the table for observation.

"This is unbelievable," an officer uttered.

The slime slurped in its container as it expanded and released a puff of orange dust. We all backed away.

"So, say this is true, how do we use this information?" asked Dean to no one in particular.

"We must only speak in truths," I said.

"And how would we mandate that exactly? We have freedom of speech." Dean scratched the side of his cheek, his eyes averted.

"What is more valued? Life or freedom?" I asked.

"I think that is for the people to decide."

"So now what? What are you going to do with this information?" I asked, impatient for movement. I wondered more than that but limited my speech. How do we disseminate this information? How do we ensure equal access? How do we mandate compliance? They could first leverage the current policing network to spread the word. From there functioning radio stations could be used to spread to a wider audience. All vehicles and men could be on patrol, announcing the news and passing out fliers. Yet as each moment passed, more died without knowing that a potential solution had been formed.

"Yeah, we'll add it to the pile." The man turned and threw the notes he had been taking on a stack of messy paperwork that had consumed his desk. He tipped his hat and escorted me out.

Chapter 20

had not been the only one to discover these characteristics. But with communication down, it felt as if the world's fate had been put into my hands. Even with some pockets armed with this key information to prevent the spread of the growth, information could only spread so quickly. And I had no further insight since handing off the information to the police and Ruth.

But this day, testing had become available, and I had no idea what to expect. Would people get tested? What will they do with the results? If I'm positive what do I do? Still, I woke up early to join the line. The socially distanced line wrapped around the building but was still shorter than I had prepared myself for. I waited about three hours to enter the building. There were a few police officers stationed inside the pharmacy, and I watched the pattern of patients going to and from the curtained room. I noticed that some that went in, didn't come out.

When my turn came, I stepped behind the curtain and a nurse dressed in a makeshift plastic suit asked me to sit. She placed a wide strap around my arm, and then two thinner ones around my chest. From these straps came numerous wires which connected back to the computer. She asked me to sit back and tilt my head upwards facing the ceiling. I opened my eyes wide, as she leaned forward and dropped a liquid into each eye. She then stared into my eyes with an intensity reserved for intimacy. But it wasn't me she was looking at—it was the surface of my eyes.

"How does this work exactly?" I asked.

"The eyes are the window to the soul." She smiled. "You will repeat true and false phrases, which will be tracked by the monitors. The monitors measure heart rate, body temperature, breathing rate, and skin conductivity. The eye drops exasperate any ophthalmological reactions, from which we can discern an infection."

"How accurate is it?"

"Fairly. Now look at me, and state 'I do not have Emissary Orange.'"

"I do not have Emissary Orange."

The nurse leaned forward with a light and magnifier, blinding me as she scanned my eyes. A steady beeping noise filled the space.

"Now repeat after me. 'I have Emissary Orange.'"

"I have Emissary Orange."

The beeping continued, but more erratically. My eyes began to water as the nurse observed them.

"You are negative."

I thanked her, and she gave me documentation. I exited out of the curtain, then the pharmacy, and out onto the street. Instead of heading straight back, I walked toward the capital with the intent of continuing towards the park. Yet as I approached the white, marbled structures of the government buildings, I could discern dark spots crawling up the pillars and walls like giant ants. There was a dark pool at the base of the building, swarming. As I drew closer, the insects morphed into people, and I could see them frantically climbing as they attempted to gain access through some of the exposed higher windows. I could hear sirens and chaotic shouting.

CHAPTER 20

Ahead of me, where the crowd was thinner, I saw a man shirtless with a fox head mounted atop his own. He snarled and howled into the crowd, waving an American flag. His face was painted red, which, coupled with the wide-open mouth of the fox, teeth rearing, looked like blood. I discerned nearby chanting, "Kill him with his own gun". Another group boasted shirts with giant swastikas. Otherwise, it was a sea of camouflage, army green, and tan——but also orange. This was no protest.

A large bang rang out, and smoke billowed from amidst the crowd. The crowd surged outward, and fear surged inside of me. It felt lawless and wild. Later images and video would surface of those breaching the capital. Men and women, armed and aligned, taking the honored seats of government to both indulge in a once-in-a-lifetime photo op, as well as to threaten those who disagree. They had accomplished what other foreign terrorists had been unable to do, by the power of underestimation and racism. I thought back to the peaceful protests for Black Lives Matter and contrasted its comradery and hope with the aggression and rage of this mob. I thought back to the Women's March on Washington, and how peacefully the protestors communicated their message.

As I backed away, I took a closer look at the orange fizzing and popping in pockets on the streets, signs, and posts. It was the most orange I had seen in any area before. Its growth was perceptible to the naked eye. I wanted to warn these people of their plight, the danger they had put themselves in spreading these falsities. Yet they felt justified in their reproach, to them this was the truth. Cayden could not help them, even with the knowledge he had acquired about the growth. He knew some people just couldn't be helped.

Chapter 21

n time, the community was able to spread the information, though it changed as it was heard. In order to provide better, more succinct guidance, a phrase was chosen to repeat which seemed to guarantee results. This phrase became "I am human." Something true to us all. Loudspeakers were set up in areas of high orange volume, repeating this phrase endlessly. Radio stations stopped most other reporting and did the same. The mass effect was discouraging, though. Countries with the worst dusting occurrences were the fastest to diminish the growth, given the forced acquiescence. Where it globed and slimed, the infections shifted rather than expired. Areas that already were troublesome grew worse, while areas already taking precautions displayed diminished cases. In time, heat maps would be created to show the effects, causing the United States to light up in luminescent swirls of orange.

Hope had once again tempted the local communities to reopen their doors. Armed with testing and this new information, though unverified, many felt a new false sense of security. This included officials. Announcements and fliers broadcasted a slow reopening, beginning with train service in and out of the city. While no official celebration was planned out of caution, various rumors of festivities spread. Most had hoped for a grand reopening, but instead, the overture was a slow burn.

I couldn't help the urge to join or at least observe. The pestilence was by no means eradicated, but a glimmer of hope was worth embracing. As I walked to the station, there was a current of individuals all being pulled toward the station as if by magnetic force. Each person an individual arrow vectoring. It was crowded in scattered density. Most wore masks, but some threw them up in the air in celebration as if it were a party hat. Music contested the stereo police declarations to remain calm and distanced.

As I walked downtown, I was tempted to forget about Emissary Orange and to throw upward my mask in victory. I didn't have the virus and I understood how to avoid it. Yet, it was unclear as to if I could still spread it. Still, I couldn't help but feel the bursting joy of hope throbbing with the crowd. Cheers were erupting, music being carried, and a sense of survivor comradery. A man behind me slapped my shoulder and wooed to the sky. The city felt alive again as if it had been resuscitated by the breath of hope.

When the train arrived, the tooting horn silenced the crowd and onlookers shifted their attention from their merriment to the arrival. Riders hung out of the windows, waving to the crowd. Names were yelled out by those trying to reconnect with loved ones after the long separation. The doors slid open and out the passengers poured. In the crowd, I recognized the news reporter from Boulder. His eyes were full of tears and his hands covered his mouth. I followed his stare, seeing a woman, reacting similarly deboarding the train. The two pushed and ran through the crowd toward each other, reuniting in a passionate embrace.

Around me, families and friends were being reunited. Couples danced in the street, swirling recklessly with overjoyed expressions. Yet the infection's presence made itself known in those who kept scanning the crowd worriedly, hoping their loved ones had found their way home only to finally embrace what they feared the most—that they too had now lost loved ones to the plague. It was confirmation of the fear that the long silence had already implanted in their hearts. Some had new grief, others confirmed old griefs. The tears, the excitement, the passion, and the sorrow all swirled like gust-driven leaves around the train terminal. Everyone seemed to feel things so much stronger than me. I began to back away and exited the station.

On turning out of the main thoroughfares where rejoice was in full swing, entering the street where Simon and Lua lived, I was held up by police presence. Sounds of festivities rang in the distance, but this street felt unusually still. Police had surrounded the entrance of Simon and Lua's apartment and were armed facing up toward the third floor. Simon and Lua lived on the third floor, facing that street where I stood.

"Sorry, but I can't let you go any further," a policeman said, "I cannot let you through. There is a crazed man with a gun, shooting at everything."

"Do you know who it is? My friends live on that floor," I asked. It couldn't be.

"Who is your friend?" the officer said as he pulled out a notepad and adjusted his belt.

"Simon Hommer and Lua Dautres. They are on that floor. Is anyone hurt?"

"Not yet."

A gunshot rang out and Simon was hanging out of the window yelling. He flailed around the gun aimlessly.

"I have my rights!" he cried.

The police officers formed a line, preventing a small crowd from drawing further near. It was eerily quiet for the number of people present. A squirrel, the first squirrel I had seen for many months, darted forward, and scrambled up a nearby tree. The branches shook and leaves rustled until a shot rang out. The bloody mass of squirrels fell to the ground. Simon had killed it in one shot.

Simon's attention was turned back inward, and I could see officers rushing toward him. I could only see the scrambled movement of limbs and bodies, unable to discern more. Gunshots fired from inside, and then a muffled denotation. At the same moment, three police officers charged across the lawn entering the lobby. And as if by signal, windows on the street were swung open and out with excited and concerned faces. The small crowd jostled forward toward the police line.

"It's Simon! He's lost it!" I cried to no one at all.

A small, surging group appeared in the lobby from the stairs. I fell, crumpled on the ground. I could not believe it. I speculated as to how we could have gotten here, how this could be. Simon had thrived during this plague, cultivating and processing the orange for recreational consumption. Perhaps he rejected the return to regularity, having grown comfortable in this new norm. The orange had forced upon him a detachment which he couldn't extract nor prevent from haunting. The illness had ended too abruptly, and he hadn't had enough time to get his act together. Happiness was bearing down on him as he thought that all would be restored. Tomorrow real life would begin, with its restrictions and the plague would not come and go without changing their hearts.

I sat myself up on the curb and waited for the nausea to pass regaining composure. In the meantime, the police dragged out Simon kicking and yelling. His mouth glowed orange as the group passed in front of me, heading to the police vehicle. I watched as they drove off, and as the dusk settled in. The once quiet street was now overcrowded with voyeurs and merrymakers. With so much hope, there was still so much pain.

Chapter 22

As I reminisce about that year, my chest grows tight. In time communications were restored, and humanity was reunited. Russian intelligence was to blame for the outage and the infection was cultivated first in bats, spreading from unsanitary raw meat markets in Asia. But for those others who aspired beyond and above the human individual toward something they could not even imagine, there had been no answer.

Studies now show that the Emissary Orange took the form of tight rigid identical cells in those places where equality and commonality was valued. Where freedom prevailed, the creature took on its amorphous unique form. However, it only formed in areas where these values had been taken too far. In China, the Orange had taken on the form of a fine powder due to communism crushing choice in the name of fairness. In the United States, it took on gradients of goo and dust, morphing as the cities gave way to more rural counties, as the populace leveraged freedom to justify mistreatment and disunion. All countries had experienced their own variety of the illness, for no one had perfected the delicate balance between liberty and fairness.

Just as the absurd is ever-present, Emissary Orange did not completely subside. When the first news of truth being a tool to diminish Emissary affects broke, many further dug in their heels in their devotion to their own truth. Most thought they were right and speaking the truth already, taking to the streets immediately under an immunity assumption. In the meantime, many still lay sick in bed, feeling the still very real effects of the orange.

The orange cloud that weighed upon us all had a silver lining though. While devastatingly deadly, it did serve to bring to the forefront more serious, universal concerns of humanity, taking precedence from the political divides that had ravaged the country. At the reopening of the town, there were no signs of a divided nation. No one wore red or blue in allegiance to their political cult. Instead, they linked arms with their neighbor, celebrating that there was more to admire in men than despise. But like hatred and division, orange was not eradicated. It instead hibernated. It can lie dormant for years in furniture and linen-chests; it bides its time in bedrooms, cellars, trunks, and bookshelves. But what is a plague, besides life itself?

In politics, the opponent won the election fairly and with a margin. The new Authority was already sworn in by the time the communication outage lifted in Denver. And the day that communications were reestablished, there was an eerie stillness that differentiated the news reports from what we had been used to hearing over the past four years. The anger that had manifested itself in political discourse had been replaced with lighthearted anecdotes. The former right reported on soft news, stories about sports and adoptions, in between updates of the infection. The former left reported on policy, which felt refreshingly dull and nuanced.

The former Authority combined steroidal treatments with the supposed truth serum. Yet when he said, "I am human," the growth did not subside but instead flourished. For this man, was not that, but instead a monster. To this day Emissary Orange grows thick on the authoritarian portrait, but blends in as if creating a three-dimensional art piece given the past Authority's carroty complexion.

One day they would build some memorial of the injustice and outrage done, such that the lessons might endure. Of knowing becomes remembered, and we mustn't forget. Terrible months taught us prudence. The plague had imbued with us a skepticism so thorough it was no second nature, allergic to hope in any form. I thought of those who I had lost or had been broken by the plague. Ruth lost her son, Simon lost his mind, Sophie lost her life, and Evie lost her hope. The combination of political unrest, economic hardship, widespread misinformation, systemic prejudice, and Emissary Orange had created a year without a future.

I extracted what I could from the year of solitude, fear, and instability. Balancing opposites, we must not give way to the absurd. While science cannot help us define our truths, it is a tool to arrange concepts that makes all the aspects of experience immediately compatible and compossible. Science is necessary, for it marks out the boundaries of knowledge and helps philosophy to avoid speculating in error. We must embrace the fearful burden of choice and disallow the quiet humble happiness of weak creatures.

The discussion of truth and authenticity was thrust center stage in the minds of the general populace, for it was no longer just philosophy but more a vaccine. We would come to find, in time, that there is no way to escape the absurd and nausea. It had become even more essential for the human experience; in that, it was the cure to the plague.

CPSIA information can be obtained
at www.ICGtesting.com
Printed in the USA
BVHW041228210222
629667BV00014B/733